THE
PHILATELIST

D.H. Coop

Fulton Books, Inc.
Meadville, PA

Published by Fulton Books 2020

ISBN 978-1-64654-667-1 (paperback)
ISBN 978-1-64654-668-8 (digital)

Printed in the United States of America

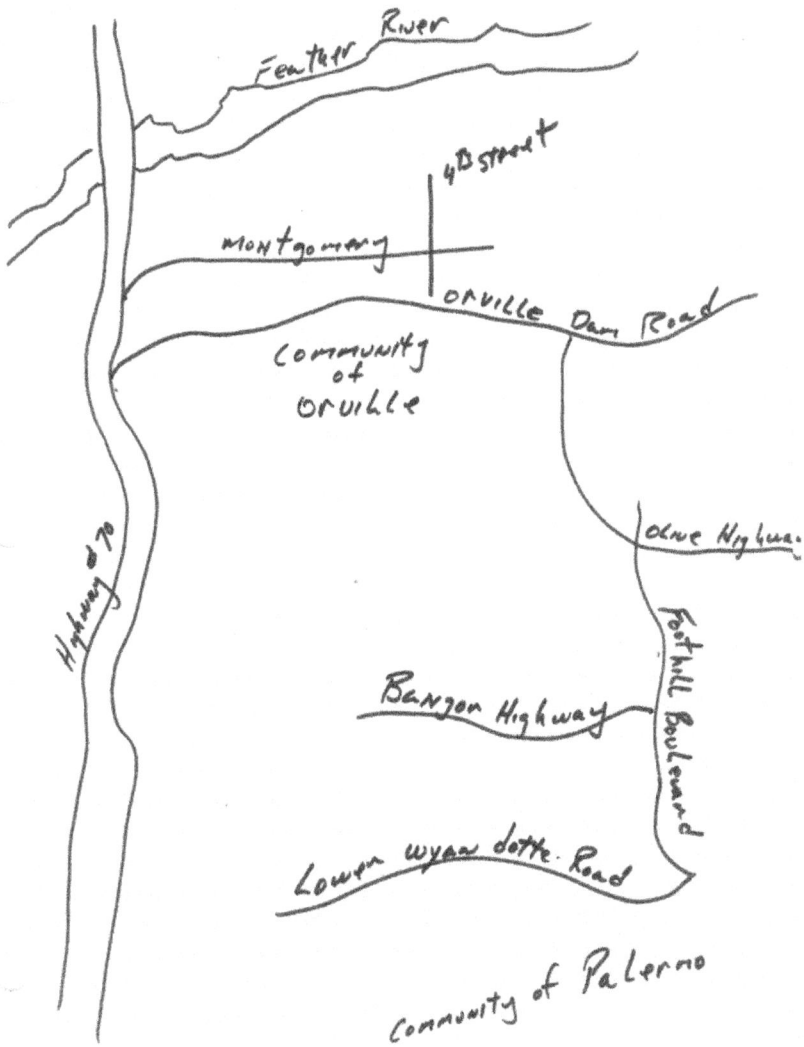

Chapter 1

Hasbrouck House, Newburgh, New York—issued April 19, 1933

This was the first stamp issued under Franklin Delano Roosevelt.

The Hasbrouck House is the location where General George Washington ordered the cessation of hostilities with Great Britain on 1783, ending the American Revolution.

August 2, 2001, 1:35 p.m.—Oroville, California

It was an unbearably hot day, one of those days when you sweat just sitting in the shade. The greenish-brown grass stood motionless in the dry heat of the sweltering afternoon sun. Stan Larson did not want to get out of his air-conditioned car although he knew he must. He hated summer because on days like this, his glasses were always slipping down over the beads of perspiration that covered his nose. So Stan delayed getting out of the car, brooding in silence, staring at the house. *Where was the old woman? She was usually standing by the front door by now, hands on her hips.*

The deferred maintenance of the outside grounds gave the house an unlived in appearance. Reluctantly, he reached toward the ignition key and turned off the engine. Opening the car door, he was greeted by the waiting heat, and almost immediately he had to push his glasses back up on his nose. "Damn tenants!" he mumbled under his breath as he shut the car door. His mood was not getting any better.

The path to the house was about thirty yards and most of it in the bright sunlight missing the shade of massive oak trees around the yard. He would have walked in the shade except the grass was filled with rice fleas (seeds with little barbs that stick to clothes) and foxtails (dart like seed quills) that would cling and work into socks and pants. He could see the heat radiating from the long cement walkway as he headed toward the porch. Stan glanced at the foxtails and rice fleas and then down at his pant legs. He resigned himself to the walkway and looked again toward the porch. *Where could she be? She knew I was coming today...*

By the time he reached the door, his shirt was wet, and his glasses had slipped down once more. Still no old woman. *Where the hell could she be?* Stan banged loudly on the door, tapping his foot impatiently. He stepped back off the porch and stood with his hands on his hips and looked around shaking his head. *She knew I would be coming today as always to collect the rent. Maybe she had forgotten. But I'll be damned if I'm going to drive all the way out here for nothing.*

He headed toward the back door of the house. Yellowed blinds covered the windows, obscuring his view as he tried to peer inside. Grasshoppers jumped around his feet as he tried to skirt the foxtails. He bent over to pull a burr from his socks and noticed that one of the blinds was broken, providing a small opening. He cupped his hands around his eyes and pressed his face close to the window.

Stan could see someone sitting in a high-backed chair facing away from him. He knocked loudly on the window and hollered. "Heidi? Heidi! Open the door!" Still no response.

"Damn tenants!" Stan said again, this time a bit more loudly. He continued to move toward the back door.

Stan Larson was a man of property. He had made a good living down south in the Los Angeles area as a real estate broker and had amassed quite a few properties. There was definitely money to be made in real estate, especially when he could collect on both sides of the deal. Stan was known for holding offers until he could line up his own clients and then tailoring the offers to cut the other agent out. But his best moneymaker was pocket listings, which he would hold until he had a client or snaked one. To Stan, business was business. If he cut someone out of a deal, he was the better businessman.

Traffic and housing laws pushed Stan north to Oroville in the early 1970s. He was tired of renting to people he didn't like. At least in the northern part of the state, the rental pool was more to his preference. He owned several rental homes and spent most of his time checking on his no-good tenants. Now in his seventies, still tall and thin, he had developed a slight bend to his posture as he walked and his personality had not improved with age. While it was not really the good life he had hoped for, it was a comfortable living.

Stan did not tolerate late rental payments and was prepared to personally collect, if necessary. On more than one occasion, he had been known to demand cash even if this meant escorting the tenant to the bank to get the money. He was certainly not going to let an old woman get out of paying her rent by ignoring him.

Heidi Miller had lived in the house for the past five years and had never been late on the rent. Whenever Stan came to check on the property, she had met him on the porch, hands on her hips, greeting him with her thick German accent. Stan realized he knew very little about her.

He'd never seen any family around, just Heidi. And their small talk about the weather and the property had only yielded one bit of personal information—she was a Holocaust survivor. He'd shown a bit of extra kindness after learning this. "And this is how she repays me!" Stan grumbled.

As Stan approached the back porch, he felt another foxtail pricking through his sock. "Damn it!" he mumbled again, reaching into his pocket for the keys. "These people never quit trying to take advantage of my good nature." He marched toward the front door, leaving a trail of grasshoppers behind him.

Stan pulled on the handle of the screen door, causing it to open with a loud pop as the rusty springs gave way. "Heidi? It's Stan Larson," he yelled. "I'm coming in!" He flipped the keys on his keychain and inserted the correct one into the lock. Though Stan had quite a collection of keys, he also had an uncanny ability to know the right key for every lock. "Your rent is late!"

Stan jiggled the key in the old lock until it turned. Then he pushed his glasses back up on his nose as he pushed the door open slightly. Immediately, an unmistakable stench caused him to recoil back onto the porch. Stan wiped the sweat from his forehead with the sleeve of his shirt and stepped into the house.

Heidi Miller was dead, and she had been that way for some time. She was sitting on her overstuffed red chair facing the front door and seemed to stare back at Stan with large dilated eyes. Her grayish white arms lay limp on the armrests of the chair. The lower part of her forearms, where they touched the chair, had a strange purplish hue where gravity had pooled the blood. It gave her arms an unworldly look. Stan took a good look to be sure and then rushed out of the house into the fresh, hot air.

His time in Los Angeles had prepared him for this type of situation. This was not the first time he had found a dead tenant—and it would probably not be the last. He took out his handkerchief and held it tightly over his nose and mouth as he went into the house again, letting the screen door slam behind him. Stan looked around at the sparse furnishings. Other than a stack of newspapers by the chair, there was little else in the room. Heidi obviously was not one to keep mementos.

Stan did not care to waste time with pity. The rent had not been paid, and now it looked as if he would lose the rent altogether unless he found some cash or anything of value he could sell.

The well-kept house reminded him of his grandmother's home. She had come from the old country, like Heidi. In a small bookcase, there were some worn books in German, and over the small mantle were a couple of beer steins. He could not help thinking that, if not for the smell of death, the stale air would probably smell like his grandmother too. Funny, but this was the first time he had entered this house in five years, and it was almost familiar.

Stan entered the bedroom and strode toward the nightstand. For some reason, people often kept their valuables near their beds; however, this time he was disappointed. Continuing through the other rooms, he could find nothing that could be turned into a quick sale to cover the rent. Just as he was about to give up and walk out, Stan noticed a blue binder that was different from the other books in the small bookcase. Removing it, he discovered that it was a well-worn Scott's International Stamp Album with mostly German, North African, and South American stamps, with a few United States stamps thrown in. Stan was no expert, but this looked more valuable than anything else in the house. Though it might not cover the rent, it was better than nothing at all.

Tucking the album under his arm, he walked out toward his car and dropped the album into the trunk. Stan looked at his watch. Nearly 2:00 p.m. He pushed the glasses up once more. It was hard to believe it could get any hotter, but the heat was rising. A fly landed on his arm, and Stan slapped it dead. Then he turned toward the house again. *The sooner I get this over with, the sooner I can get back into my air-conditioned car,* he thought. He walked back to the house and found the phone.

"Yes, um, hello, operator. Could you get me the sheriff's department?"

"Sir, is this an emergency?"

"No, I am just reporting a death."

"Are you being sarcastic, sir?"

"No! The individual has been dead for some time."

"One moment, please."

Stan heard a click as the phone was transferred to the sheriff's office and a stern voice greeted him. "This is Sargent Allen, how can I help you?"

"This is Stan Larson, and I am at a place I own on Foothill, where Heidi Miller lives. She is dead, so you'd better send out a unit!"

The stern voice prodded him with a few questions.

"What? No, I found her sitting in her chair... Yes, she's definitely dead... No, I haven't touched anything inside the house... Sure, I will be glad to stay here until the unit arrives. Thank you."

Stan waited on the front porch. It was just as hot in the house, and there was the unbearable smell to contend with inside.

Chapter 2

Fort Dearborn—issued May 25, 1933

Franklin Delano Roosevelt approved this stamp to commemorate the Century of Progress World Fair in Chicago.

August 2, 2001, at 3:27 p.m.—Oroville, California

It had taken quite a while for Deputy Hoff to take Stan's statement of how he found Heidi's body. The deputy took careful notes, asked a few more questions, and thanked Stan for his cooperation. Then the deputy entered the house. Stan paused and peered through the screen as the deputy looked around the living room. He watched the deputy touch the bookcase and examine the dust-free spot where the binder had been. Then Stan strode toward his car.

Stan's white shirt now had large sweat stains under the arms and in the front and back, exposing his sleeveless undershirt. Starting the car, Stan stepped back out onto the driveway to allow the air-conditioning to cool the inside of the car. He pulled his sticky undershirt away from his chest and pushed the glasses up on his nose once more. Then he sighed and sat down on the car seat.

As he drove away, Stan wondered how long it was going to take to rent the house this time. *Do I have to disclose the death to the next tenant?* As he recalled, the law said you had to disclose a death when you sold a place, not when you rented one. *But what if someone gets wind of this?* People could be funny, and some might have a problem renting a house where someone had recently died. *Damn,* he thought, *did she really have to go and die now when I already had another vacancy?*

It was a good thing he had taken that album. What was she going to do with it anyway? She didn't have any family that he knew of. And she owed him for the rent. He reached up with his fingers to push the glasses back into place.

The air-conditioning kicked into high gear, and he turned his face toward the blast of cool air coming from the vents. Then he put the car into drive and turned left onto Foothill Boulevard and headed toward town. He decided to stop by Ed's Coin & Stamp on the way home to unload the album.

Detouring onto Montgomery Street, he headed straight for Fourth Street and was pleased to see a parking space right in the front of the store. At least something was going right. Stan sat in the car for a minute or two thinking about what he would tell Ed. Stan had learned that the best lies were the ones that made a connection for the person being lied to. The story had to have an element of personal truth—something that most people had experienced at some time in their lives. It was even better if that experience had a measure of guilt connected with it. Everyone had a grandmother or aunt they remembered, so Stan would pull out the grandmother's story with the album. He got out of the car, opened the trunk, grabbed the album, and headed for the front door of the store, hoping it would be air-conditioned.

Chapter 3

National Recovery Act—issued August 15, 1933

This stamp was used to advertise the cornerstone of Franklin Delano Roosevelt's New Deal.

August 2, 2001, at 4:07 p.m.—Oroville, California

Ed Hegel was a short balding man with a large waist. He was always looking for that one "big deal" in his life. Anyone looking at Ed would think he was completely broke. He drove an old broken-down car and wore the shabbiest of clothes that did not appear to have been washed all that recently. Clients would sometimes give him items for free when he was called out to appraise something because he seemed to need the money more than they did.

The little bell at the door sounded to announce Stan's entrance. Sitting at the counter, Ed looked up from his coin magazine and smiled.

"Hey, Stan! What can I do for you today? Have you decided to become a coin collector?"

"Nah," laughed Stan. "I just found this old stamp album of my grandmother's in the attic and figured I might as well get rid of it, you know? It's the collector, not me. Dust collector that is!"

"Well, let me have a look," Ed said with a chuckle as he reached for the blue book.

Stan watched as Ed went through the book in a hurry, as if it was of little importance to him. After a few pages, Ed even began flipping through groups of pages at a time. Stan knew that Ed's expertise was really in coins. But in a small town, one had to sell in general areas to stay in business.

Though his knowledge was mostly superficial, Stan knew a few things about stamps. Airmails, for example, were a good buy because of their high starting value and their limited circulation. And air travel had been limited for most of the century, making them even more unusual.

Stan looked expectantly at Ed as he leafed through the pages, pausing on the German and airmail stamps. As he neared the end of the book, Ed studied the last page for a moment and then looked up.

"I will give you one thousand and five hundred dollars for it as is," Ed pronounced as he shut the book.

"One thousand and five hundred dollars?" repeated a surprised Stan. He had not expected nearly that much. That was nearly double what he was owed in rent.

"You might get more for it if you took it over to the Bay Area, but I doubt it," said Ed.

"Your offer sounds fair to me," Stan said. He felt a pang of guilt but quickly reminded himself that the extra money would make up for the lost rent while he was looking for a new tenant.

Ed moved toward the cash register and carefully counted out $1,500 in a combination of twenties and one-hundred-dollar bills.

"Thanks, Ed," Stan said. "I have got to run, but I will see you around!"

After Stan pulled away from the curb to head back to Palermo, Ed looked out the shop window. "Did I offer too much?" he said aloud to himself. "Stan doesn't usually take a deal unless he thinks it's a good one. Maybe the book isn't worth the three thousand dollars I hope it is." As Stan pulled away, he waved. Then he sat down and continued to flip through the coin catalog.

Chapter 4

Century of Progress (airmail)—issued October 2, 1933

Known as the Baby Zeppelin.

The post office worked with the Graf Zeppelin Company in a plan to bring attention to the Exposition in Chicago with a special postage stamp. The Postal Service estimated $10,000 in revenue from the sale of the stamps. FDR refused to allow the stamp. A diplomatic incident was avoided when FDR allowed the agreement to continue.

August 2, 2001, at 4:54 p.m.—Oroville, California

The afternoon had been slow, as usual, except for Stan. Just as Ed was about to close up shop for the day, the bell on the door rang, and a tall customer walked into the store. Ed appeared out of the back room to see who it was.

"Can I help you?" asked Ed, not recognizing the customer.

"I am just passing through town and saw your shop," said the man. "I am somewhat of a novice stamp collector and thought you just might have something of interest for me."

Ed looked over to the end of the counter where the blue international album still lay. He moved his head in the general direction. "There is this one album I was preparing for display that might interest you."

Both men moved to the end of the counter to look at the book in question. Ed sized up the man and surmised that he probably had some money. Although not ostentatious, he was neatly groomed. *Probably from San Francisco,* Ed thought. *I might want to start with a higher price.*

"This is one of my more prized collections," Ed boasted as if he were the proud daddy of a new baby. Ed lowered his voice and continued conspiratorially, "I had planned on selling the stamps individually, but if it interests you, I might be persuaded to sell it as a package."

The stranger picked up the album and looked through it carefully. Ed looked at the clock on the wall. Although it had been a long day, Ed would wait until midnight to make a sale. After a few minutes, the stranger put down the book and asked Ed for the price.

"I could let you have it as a set for five thousand dollars," Ed said, trying to be matter of fact. Hoping the price had not been too high to scare the customer off. Yet, if he could sell it at that price he would have a quick profit of $3500 with no wasted time pricing the stamps.

The tall man stood silently for what seemed to Ed like an eternity. Then he responded, "That is more than I wanted to spend, but you have a sale. Will you take a check?"

"Absolutely!" Ed answered, trying not to give away his excitement.

The stranger pulled out his leather checkbook and made out the check. So as not to offend his wealthy customer, Ed took the check and did not ask for any identification or references. "Thank you for your business, Mr. Hall," Ed said. The customer picked up the stamp album and walked out of the store. Ed neglected to make a record of the purchase.

The stranger smiled as he got into his car, as though he felt pleased with his purchase. He leafed through the album briefly. Not only would some of the stamps fit nicely into his album at home, he figured there must be over $50,000 retail value in stamps in the album. Then he started his car and pulled out, smiling broadly. There is still gold in these little towns.

Ed again stood at the window and watched his good fortune drive away. Then we walked out the door and locked it, once again feeling cheated. *He jumped at my first offer!* Ed scolded himself. *When will I ever learn? But I did make a tidy profit. Maybe I'll treat myself to dinner at Greta's!*

Chapter 5

Mother's Day—issued May 2, 1934

Franklin Delano Roosevelt and Postmaster General Farley designed a stamp in honor of James Abbott McNeill Whistler's hundredth anniversary and to honor Mother's Day.

The words on the stamp are the president's.

August 2, 2001, at 9:12 p.m.—Bangor Highway

This evening was less tiresome than usual. At dinner, Ed convinced himself that the price was too low—he had actually sold the album to a sucker. By the end of his fifth beer, he actually believed the story. He even told it to his favorite waitress, Carlene, hoping to impress her. She always waited on Ed when he came in to eat. He noticed that she seemed to flirt with him, and he thought often of asking her out on a date. But he had never had the nerve. He was sure she was out of his league.

Ed was thinking of this when Carlene stopped at the table and stared at him in a strange way. "Ed, this may be forward of me," she said, "but I don't care. I like you, and I think you like me so why don't we go out some night?"

Carlene was not tall, and her figure looked attractive, even in the pink waitress dress that clashed with her red dyed hair and bright ruby-red nails. Trying to hide his shock, Ed stumbled over his words as he responded, "Carlene, I would very much like to take you out on a date. How about tomorrow night?"

"That would be fine with me, Ed. I am glad I broke the ice! You can pick me up at seven. Here is the address. I'll see you tomorrow then."

"Great, we can go over to Chico and dance at that country western club by the college…if that's okay with you."

"That is wonderful! I love to dance," Carlene said as Ed walked toward the door. Her eyes followed him as he crossed the street and got into his car. She wondered what Ed would wear…surely not his normal old clothes.

The drive home was short and lonely out on Bangor Highway to Ed's ten acres. By the time he pulled into the drive of his home, the daylight was almost gone, and shadows were cast about the yard. Walking up to his door, he was met by two men in dark-blue suits, who appeared out of the shadows. One was tall, and the other quite short. After the initial shock of seeing them come out of nowhere, Ed relaxed a little bit. They looked official—not like the kind to cause trouble.

"Who the hell are you guys?" asked Ed.

"Are you the owner of the coin store in town?" the taller man, asked ignoring Ed's question.

"Yes, I am," replied Ed. "And who are you?"

"Did Stan Larson sell you a stamp album earlier today?" asked the shorter man, again ignoring Ed's question.

"Who wants to know?" asked Ed suspiciously, wondering what Stan had gotten him into with the album.

"Just answer the question," replied the taller man, again in a forceful tone, which caused Ed to take a step back.

"Yes, and I paid a fair price too," Ed said defensively. "Listen, you guys, I do not know who you are or what this is about. But I'm not going to stand here and talk with you about this any longer until I see some identification."

The taller man produced a black leather case from his inside coat pocket and held it out to Ed. As Ed stepped forward to take a look at the wallet, he didn't notice the smaller man's move. The pain was brief…and then the darkness came.

Chapter 6

Connecticut Tercentenary—issued April 26, 1935

When Sir Edmund Andros, under the authority of King James, attempted to seize the charter of the Connecticut colony, the colonists took the charter into the woods and hid it in an old oak tree for two years until Andros was recalled. Franklin Delano Roosevelt suggested the "rich lilac" color.

August 3, 2001, at 6:45 a.m.—Oroville, California

As the assistant manager, Carlene was training a new waitress on the fine art of waitress shorthand when she was interrupted.

"Hey, Carlene," called one of the regular morning customers.

"What do you want Ralph?" asked Carlene irritably. "Don't you see that I'm busy?"

"Have you seen the paper? It is about Ed. You know, Ed Hegel." Ralph was insistent and pushed the paper toward Carlene. She picked it up and put her hand over her mouth to stifle a scream as she collapsed to the floor. The local newspaper headline read:

COIN DEALER MURDERED AND ROBBED

Local coin dealer Ed Hegel was found murdered at his home late last night. A neighbor's dog was barking for an unusual length of time, and the neighbor went to investigate. He found Mr. Hegel's body lying outside around 11:00 p.m. It is believed that he was killed during a robbery attempt at his home, which had been burglarized. The killer or killers used Mr. Hegel's keys to enter and rob his coin store. The store was unlocked, and the keys were left in the alarm in the off position. The sheriff's department will not comment, but inside sources report that they have no leads at this time.

On page 2 the following story was reported:

Local Homeowner Falls Downstairs

Stan Larson, local real estate agent and landlord, died yesterday. Mr. Larson apparently fell down his basement staircase and broke his neck. He was found by a friend. Funeral arrangements are pending.

On page 8, the obituary column listed:

Heidi Miller, born in Germany in 1920, was discovered dead at her home yesterday afternoon by Stan Larson, her landlord. She had no known relatives. Ms. Miller escaped from a Nazi concentration camp in 1938 before fleeing to the United States. She had lived in Oroville since 1946. Cause of death is unknown but is presumed to be heart failure.

Chapter 7

Shield Bearer—issued March 3, 1937

German Shield Bearers were formed to train civilians for protection from air raids.

March 17, 1945, at 2:45 a.m.—off the coast of Santa Barbara, California

The U-Boat broke the gentle, rolling surface of the sea in the moonless night with only a slight offshore breeze. The swells made a rhythmic slapping sound against the U-Boat's low silhouette. It would be difficult to distinguish the boat from either sea or shore, even if there were a moon out. Before the seawater had drained off the hull, men silently began to emerge from the interior of the vessel. Each man moved quickly to his assigned station without the need for spoken orders. Lookouts scanned the black sky and dark horizon for the sight of any enemy who might have noticed their metal sea monster. Should they give the alarm, the men would go scurrying back into the hatches and slip quickly and silently back into the depths of the sea from which they had come.

After a few minutes, the only sound that could be heard was that of the waves breaking on the distant shoreline. They had surfaced close enough to the beach to hear the surf breaking on the sand and rocks of the Santa Barbara coastline. As they slowly moved toward the land, the sound grew perceptibly louder. With no moon in the cloudless sky to give away their position, the men sat confidently, as though the war was theirs to win.

The kapitän climbed up the ladder to the top of the con and drew a long, deep breath of fresh Pacific Ocean air, enjoying the refreshing bite of the breeze in the early hours of the morning. No matter how often or how long at sea, he never grew tired of the smell of the ocean and its refreshing bite of air in the early morning hours. With a keen eye, he scanned the deck, inspecting his crew. Then he leaned forward on the gray metal railing and allowed his thoughts to wander, satisfied that everything was in order, as always. His thoughts wondered over the events of the past few weeks and the momentous journey they had just completed. Would this change the outcome of the war?

Chapter 8

Wehrmacht Series: U-boot Type VII—issued March 21, 1943

February 12, 1945, at dusk—near Kiel, Germany

Kapitän Reinhold von Holstein stood on the concrete platform looking at the dark clouds, which partially obscured the setting sun on the horizon. The wind made an already chilly day even colder. A North Sea wind in February was always brisk and icy, and it promised to be a cold night too. The kapitän adjusted his leather jacket, turning up the collar and pulling it together over the Iron Cross, first class, which hung at his neck. The sound of approaching voices caused him to turn.

A small group was approaching, and he only knew one of the four people winding their way down the iron stairway to the concrete platform. It was his first officer, Helmut Dorfmann. Behind them was the partially concealed concrete-reinforced submarine bunkers, which formerly held the pride of the German Navy's submarine fleet. Now many of them were bombed-out ruins, and none had escaped damage. Times had definitely changed for the worse.

When Kapitän von Holstein had been attached to the German Naval High Command in late 1938, he had participated in a study, which recommended that Germany would need at least three hundred undersea boats if they were to contest the sea lanes and defeat the English Navy in war.

However, at that time, before that the war had started, Germany had only 22 ocean-going U-Boats ready for sea duty. Yet that early optimistic assessment of 300 U-Boats had been surpassed, and just this month U-Boat production had hit 1,170. Unfortunately, of these, 784 had already been sunk, along with their crews.

"Hello, Kapitän!" Helmut enthusiastically called out as he motioned his three companions toward the platform where von Holstein awaited. Von Holstein could not help but smile at his first officer, whose good nature was always a point of pleasure for the entire crew during long tours at sea. Even now, before the dangerous and risky venture, Helmut was still in good spirits.

The kapitän waved back. Helmut was a rather short and stocky man, in stark contrast to the kapitän, who was tall and lean. The three other individuals, two men and a woman, were all of medium height with light-colored hair. The men wore black SS uniforms of the Leibenstardte Division, and the woman wore a uniform of the Death Heads SS Unit of the camps.

But what really struck von Holstein about the young men were their eyes. They had not seen the real terror of war and its effects, yet their eyes told a different story, as though they had seen a great deal of death and destruction. Of this, the kapitän was sure. The woman, on the other hand, looked at him with empty eyes, as though she felt nothing.

"Kapitän, I would like to introduce you to Sturmbannführer's Steiner, Rossmann, and Muller," said Helmut as each man clicked his heels, bowed slightly, and raised his arm in the party salute as his name was mentioned. The woman seemed remote and mechanical in her salute. *Strange,* thought von Holstein, *how a woman so beautiful was so completely devoid of emotion and the knowledge of her effect on men.*

Kapitän von Holstein saluted as a naval officer rather than return the party salute. If the three noticed this omission, they did not indicate it. Helmut preferred diplomacy and seemed slightly amused at the kapitän's choice. The two men had begun the war full of optimism, as staunch advocates of the sanctity and honor of the cause. However, that was long ago, and now their thoughts were often filled with disillusionment of leadership and war. But they would do their duty to the end. However, these two new men on the other hand were a rarity these days. They were true believers fighting for a cause. Whatever that cause was.

"It is a pleasure to make your acquaintance, Kapitän," said the one introduced as Steiner. "We have read your dossier, and it is quite impressive."

"You are too kind," replied von Holstein.

"No, you are truly a hero of the Third Reich. One of our most decorated and skilled U-Boat commanders," continued the man named Meinhoff. "We are very fortunate to have you as our commander for this mission of the Fuhrer."

"Yes, the tide has now turned on the enemies of the Fatherland," exulted Steiner.

Von Holstein nodded in agreement. *Fools,* he thought. This month, significantly more U-boats had been lost than Allied merchant ships. American and British submarine detection technology was far superior. And British and American intelligence seem to have cracked their codes. So now the hunter had become the hunted—and the Germans are paying the price in naval blood.

"Why do we not retire to the command bunker?" suggested von Holstein. "Food and drinks have been prepared so that we might enjoy a meal while we talk. Once it is dark, we shall leave."

The small party of men and the woman moved toward the metal doors a few yards away.

A small concrete opening protruded from the side of a stone cliff. The gray concrete was camouflaged with green, gray, and black markings. Two Kriegsmarine guards stood smartly to attention as the men entered the command center's outer chamber.

Though the command room was sparsely furnished, the few staff officers moved quickly about with a sense of urgency. The base was mostly empty now, but it was still subjected to both nightly and daytime bombing raids. It was best to be inside in case the air raid sirens sounded.

Leading the group into a small side conference room, von Holstein motioned for each to take a seat around an oblong wooden table. Maps, diagrams, and folding chairs were scattered about the room.

The lack of organization was one of the reasons this base had been chosen. The repair facility was no longer operational. Only three U-Boats were still operating from it, and all of them were at sea. With Germany's diminished capacity, all production and repair activities had been allocated to the larger more important facilities.

After the group was seated, von Holstein began, "I have not been informed what your mission entails, nor do I wish to know, nor should you tell me if I should ask. However, I am aware of where we will be going. No one but those of you in this room, with the exception of a few at the highest of levels, is even aware of what we will be doing. You are not to speak to the crew about the mission—either now or during our passage. Is that clear?"

"Yes, Kapitän!" the officers answered together.

"Now please help yourselves to the food. I must speak with the first officer for a moment in private." Von Holstein guided Helmut into another room and shut the door.

"Helmut, I am sorry that I have been unable to speak with you sooner about what I am going to tell you," said von Holstein. "Submerged offshore as I speak is a vessel that will forever change the way undersea warfare will be fought. It is waiting for us. As you know, our Fuhrer has always been a supreme supporter of the development of new weapons. Our naval engineers have successfully adapted a Dutch device known as a snorkel and added it to two prototype U-Boats. One is a short-range two-hundred-ton vessel, and the other is a long-range one-thousand-and-five-hundred-ton vessel. We will be using the long-range vessel known as the XXI."

"What exactly is a snorkel? And what are you talking about?" asked a puzzled Helmut.

"A snorkel is a device that will allow us to recharge our batteries without the need to surface," responded von Holstein.

"That's wonderful!" Helmut responded with glee.

"As you know, typically a U-Boat has a surface speed of just over 17 knots. Using this snorkel and other new modifications, we will be able to maintain a submerged speed of up to 18 knots."

"Are you kidding?" said Helmut with a look of disbelief on his face.

"I am dead serious, my friend."

"How is it that you are telling me now?" asked Helmut.

"I was instructed to only tell those who needed to know. But if I am lost, you must carry out the mission. I am sorry, my old friend, that I was not able to tell you sooner.

"A handpicked skeleton crew is currently on board. The remaining members of our old crew should be arriving here as we speak," von Holstein continued.

"This is unbelievable," said Helmut, still showing signs that he was somewhat mystified by what he had just learned.

"Yes, this is unbelievable," agreed von Holstein. "I hope that it will help the war effort, but I am afraid it is too late for us to claim victory now."

"The only thing left is for us to do our duty," replied Helmut.

"Yes! Our mission is one of evasion, not attack. The snorkel has been coated with antiradar materials and is fitted with radar search aerials. Our submerged speed is great enough to outrun any potential depth charge attack if we are detected. We also have on board an ultrasensitive hydrophone system, which will allow us to locate enemy ships up to fifty miles away. The supersonic echo will set the range, direction, speed, and number of targets," von Holstein said as he paced the small room, hands clasped behind his back.

"All without surfacing," marveled Helmut more to himself than his kapitän. "Furthermore, should we encounter an enemy destroyer, we will be able to switch the engines over to an electric motor with a belt drive system, which allows for silent running at under five knots. There has also been an improvement in armament capabilities, which include torpedoes able to fire at any angle from a depth of a hundred and fifty feet while still accurately tracking the target. A new zigzag and acoustic torpedo has been secretly developed. We will not be fooled by the British foxer decoys that emit sounds to foil our noise-detection torpedoes. Even the tactic of turning off the engines will not stop this new weapon."

"Unbelievable!" Helmut paused in astonishment and then began speaking again. "After we have delivered our three pieces of luggage," he said, motioning with his head toward the three officers in the next room, "will we have the opportunity to try our luck with these new devices?"

"Absolutely! But first, we must get them to the American West Coast without anyone discovering us. Now come, we must rejoin our guests in the next room."

Chapter 9

Wehrmacht Series, Pioniere—issued March 21, 1943

March 17, 1945, at 2:50 a.m.—Santa Barbara, California

Looking at the scattered blinking lights of the California coastline, the kapitän could not help but smile. With the Allied armies closing in on Germany and Japan, the Americans had become overconfident of victory. So much so that they appeared to be totally unconcerned about the possibility of invasion. True, there was never a real possibility of that occurring. But they did not know that then and disregarded it now.

Even early in the war, sightings of U-Boats off the eastern coast of America were often exaggerated or untrue. Von Holstein even heard stories of Americans believing U-Boat crews came ashore to shop for food and clothes! *What a simpleminded culture these Americans have,* he thought.

Von Holstein did remember the easy pickings of merchant marine ships off the Atlantic coast that were made easier by the foolish American Atlantic Coastal Command. Believing that the East Coast was too densely populated to suffer an invasion, they had not ordered the blackout of the resort cities until May of 1942, and this illumination had provided a fine backdrop for the sinking of merchant ships. He laughed at the memory of the frightened American Coast Guard attacking large numbers of whales, thinking they were U-Boats. Well, they had gotten better since then, that was certain. It was this early success that encouraged the later exaggeration of the stories on both sides. If only Germany had the three hundred U-boats back in 1939, England would not have survived until America came into the war.

Von Holstein gave the signal to Helmut, who was down with the gun crew.

Helmut led the gun crew over to a small rubber boat, which they were able to quickly manhandle over the side. Once it was in the water, they secured it with holding lines next to the hull before Helmut turned to motion to the kapitän that it was ready. The kapitän sent one of the lookouts down the ladder, and a few moments later, three dark figures emerged on the deck of the U-Boat near the rubber boat. They turned and gave the party salute with their right arm outstretched before climbing into the rubber boat. After they were all securely in the craft, Helmut and the others released the lines and cast the boat loose.

The entire topside crew saluted. Then, just as quickly as they had arrived, the men disappeared, and the U-Boat slid under the waves. The tiny rubber boat and its passengers headed into the night on a secret mission to save Germany.

The kapitän and crew were happy. They had crossed two oceans undetected. Now they would see how well the U-Boat performed in combat on their return trip home. Meanwhile, their three passengers were heading toward the destination that could change the course of the war.

Chapter 10

Transpacific Airmail—issued November 22, 1935

Franklin Delano Roosevelt pointed out a mistake in the design: the clipper ship on the left had only two masts instead of three. In 1937, China was added to the route, and the name of the series became China Clipper airmail.

Warm Springs, Georgia—1939

The six-room cottage was finished in 1932 at a cost of $8,738, which included a garage, servants' quarters, a guesthouse, and landscaping. The front of the cottage had a circular drive that balanced the grand entrance. A covered roof extended out from the building and was held in place by four white pillars. There was no porch from the drive to the front door. Each side of the door had two sets of windows that were rimmed with shutters. The architect Henry Toombs had done other work for the occupant of the cottage. He had designed the unusual floor plan so that it allowed the occupant, Franklin Delano Roosevelt, to move around in his wheelchair. Roosevelt had come to Warm Springs in 1924 with hopes of a cure for the effects of infantile paralysis he contracted in 1921.

The mineral waters at the Meriwether Inn had reputedly cured another victim of polio, a man who regained the use of his legs in the warm mineral waters. This expectation drew Roosevelt to buy twelve thousand acres of land close to the health spa and its healing waters for $195.

Then the governor of New York, Roosevelt began working on the cottage, which became known as the little White House when he was installed in the office of president of the United States in March 1933. The same year, Adolf Hitler assumed the position of chancellor in Germany and started his grab for complete power. He would have his escape home built later at Berchtesgaden called the Eagle's Nest.

As the world seemed to be turning away from democratic governments and moving toward authoritarian strongmen, FDR was seen by many as the man to save the nation from collapse into dictatorship. His first days in office—called the Hundred Days—saw a rush of activity and hope, reminiscent of Napoleon's escape from the island of Elba and his defeat at Waterloo in just a hundred days.

However, as time went by, the business community and members of Wall Street loathed and feared FDR. They saw new taxes as a left-wing attack on capitalism. The *Hearst* newspapers began calling the New Deal the Raw Deal, and the tax bill was labeled Soak the Rich. These business leaders feared FDR was taking America into socialism, or even communism, with his pampering of labor unions and the rise of the Young Communist camps around the country.

The conservatives began forming an alliance, including Dr. Francis Townsend, Father Coughlin of Detroit, and Senator Huey P. Long of Louisiana. This alliance began attacking the president as the capitalist kingpin who wanted to keep the little guy down.

Dr. Townsend had published an article in the *Independent Press Telegram* of Long Beach, California, in September of 1933 that offered two hundred dollars a month for every person over the age of sixty. The fact that the plan would consume half of the national budget to provide income to 9 percent of the population hit a nerve. Thousands of Townsend Clubs were formed with over two million members collecting more than twenty-five million signatures on a petition to the congress to support the Townsend Plan.

Then there was Father Charles E. Coughlin, who had been one of the first to recognize the reach of radio programming. By 1932, his audience was large enough to require over a hundred clerks and four secretaries to handle his fan mail. His program was the most listened to program at the time and was filled with proclamations of hate for Jews and big banking. By 1935, he led the campaign to stop the New Deal administration from ratifying a treaty that would make the US a member of the World Court by claiming that it was an international conspiracy of money interests that would destroy American sovereignty. As a result of Coughlin's political propaganda, the US did not join. Senator Huey P. Long, the Kingfish and the catalyst to the populist mix of anti-administration leaders, started out by selling Bibles on the road and went on to be governor and senator of the state of Louisiana, even holding both offices at the same time. He was repeatedly investigated for corruption, but no charges were ever filed. He took his Share the Wealth and Every Man a King programs to the national level and attempted to form a coalition with Townsend and Coughlin.

The far right had different plans. Teutonia in Chicago, the German Bund center with Camp Siegfried on Long Island, and the Silver Shirts in Los Angeles formed the American fascist movement. Still others worked behind closed doors to train spies and saboteurs. Their goal was corporate socialism based on the guidelines of Italy and Germany.

FDR's social legislation of 1935 weakened attacks from the left as attacks from the right picked up steam. In response to the business community turning away from his program, FDR turned to organized labor for support with the Wagner Act and Social Security Act. Then a new problem was created with the postmaster general over a simple stamp.

FDR sat in his office behind his massive desk. "Tell me again how this thing started, James, and what can we do to control it," he commanded Postmaster General James Farley.

"Well, to be honest, no good deed goes unpunished. I had a few sheets of stamps printed for friends and for you, including the National Parks imperforated stamps. Then one sheet of stamps showed up in New York. Someone tried to use the sheet with my signature on it as collateral for a loan. When collectors found out, they started yelling favoritism and demanded the same opportunity to get these Farley's follies."

"You know, James, we have to deal with this problem quickly. There is an election coming next year, and there are several individuals who want me out of office. Congress is being pulled in, and Republicans are demanding an investigation. Representative Millard of New York wants an explanation before his House committee in February."

"Yes, sir…I know. I thought this would die down and people would forget about it."

"Huey Long and his friends are going to have a heyday with this if we do not control the fallout quick."

"I will reprint the stamps in a limited number for collectors. That should quiet things down before the election campaign gets rolling, Mr. President."

"Let's hope so. I do not want to lose leverage with the unions now that business has turned away from our plan to make a society that will leave no one out."

"You know, James, that Long fellow will be a candidate like a Hitler type."

"I conducted a secret poll and it showed that as a third-party candidate, he would pull 10 percent of the voters. I am keeping an eye on the situation."

"We need to solidify the South before the election in 1936."

"I am working on it, Franklin."

The threat from the right ended with an assassin's bullet that set off a chain of events, ending the life of Kingfish on the night of September 8, 1935. Bodyguards opened fire on Carl Weiss, leaving thirty bullet holes in his front and twenty-nine bullet holes in his back. When the bodyguards were done firing, it was unclear who fired the fatal bullet that killed Huey P. Long.

Huey's death left the coalition weak and fragmented, without a strong leader to hold the personalities together. Plus, the Second New Deal found loyal support with the working man.

Year

Organization

Travel

Country

Chapter 11

Overrun Nations: Greece—issued June 22, 1943

Franklin Delano Roosevelt's desire was to keep away from militaristic themes for this series of stamps. As a result, he suggested the flag theme.

August 3, 2001, at 5:43 p.m.

Though he was given the name Clarence Ebenezer Hall at birth, he preferred CE. A self-imposed loner in a crowd, he liked being around people, but he was not fond of groups. He found the act of engaging in light conversation to be tedious, hard work. As a fireman on an engine company, he found lots of time for light conversation, and his reluctance to engage caused other firemen to see him as unsociable. It was primarily for this reason that he joined the fire investigation bureau. Finally he did not have to sit around and chat as he waited for the next run.

Almost everyone saw the fire investigators as a strange breed, like CE. But those who knew CE said he was different, even in that group. People often enjoyed his wit and dry sense of humor. A little over six feet tall, with broad shoulders and of medium weight, CE had a square face with a rugged country folk hero look. When he entered a room, his presence could be felt, not in terms of his looks, power, or wealth but rather in the way he commanded the space. CE always seemed to be in control of his surroundings.

He was now an independent fire investigator who completely enjoyed his work and was in great demand. In his spare time, CE was a philatelist who used his fire-investigation skills to sniff out the history, geography, and previous owners of the stamps in his collections. He found that stamps were not just small pieces of artwork—they also had stories behind them. He was able to relax and unwind by looking up the previous owners of collections and finding out why they were sold. In his collection, he had some stamps from Franklin Delano Roosevelt's personal collection that were traded back in the 1930s to a New York dealer. He also had some of the infamous national park stamps that Farley had reprinted for FDR. However, CE's real interest was his international collection, which is why he had purchased this new album.

Driving home on I-5 was always a hot and lonely drive, but CE took little side trips hunting for stamps to break the boredom. On one particularly hot and long trip, he was thinking about the international album he had just bought the evening before in Oroville.

Parts of it would fit nicely into his collection. The album seemed to have almost complete, never-hinged sections from Germany, Austria, Italy, Spain, North Africa, and South America, with a good selection from the United States. Most of the stamps were pre-1955.

The time passed so fast that he did not notice he had entered Los Angeles County. He reached over for his phone and called his directory for any messages. The message service told him that a Chief Benjamin Franklin had called fifteen minutes before and said he had a small job if CE was in town.

Chief Benjamin Franklin had known CE since they were rookies together. Their friendship began the day they were caught in a stairway to a basement in a backdraft explosion. Their captain had twisted his knee getting off the unit and told the two rookies to take the basement. They had rushed down the stairs in the dark and did not see the smoke being drawn back under the door. Fortunately, they had not gone five steps down when explosion hurled them both back up into the alley. They laid there for a minute, trying to figure out what had happened. The force of the explosion had pushed their facemasks off. At almost the same time, they looked at each other and smiled.

"Shit! Am I alive?"

"Wow! You're some kind of a party animal," said CE.

"Yeah, you're not so bad yourself," Franklin said. And they had been friends ever since.

CE pulled up to the location the chief had given him and got out of the car. It was a warm evening, and the neighborhood kids were out in force. The house was a California bungalow, and the neighborhood was on the way down economically from middle-class professional to hourly blue collar. He walked through the police line and around the fire rig's hose lines.

"Hi, Chief. I hear you've been looking for me."

"Where have you been? Ever since you took that medical retirement and went into private investigation, nobody can find you."

"I was up in Washington state working on a case where some guy tried to rip off his insurance company. He had a stable of prime horse-breeding stock, which he removed and replaced with broken-down horse stock. Then he piled water-reactive chemicals in the barn with the animals. He made a small hole in the roof, and all he had to do was wait for it to rain. Kind of an ingenuous plan—only the structure did not burn the way he planned. It was easy to put it together. Computers are great for looking into records. Anyway, he broke down when I showed him that we knew he had debt trouble and had the figures to prove it and that we had traced the prime horse stock to an out-of-state location."

"All that's real nice, but can we cut it short?" said the chief.

"My, my, somebody is a grouch today."

"Well, I've got a small problem here. There's a dead guy on the ground over there, and the house was almost gutted by the time we arrived on the scene. We knocked the fire down in about eight minutes, and we are only hitting hot spots now and then. The landlord wants to have an independent investigator's report. He said he did not trust the tenant, and he's mad at us for not getting here to save the building. So I guess he does not trust us either. I told him you're the best. So the job is yours, if you want it."

"Mind if I look around the house first?"

"That's what you are here for."

CE started to walk around the house. He always did his investigations in the same systematic way. As he walked around the outside, he looked for anything out of the ordinary. When he got back to the front door, he discovered what was little more than a heap of splinters with an unlocked latch still in the frame. The truckees had used their "fireman's key" to open the door—and the axe had not left much of the door intact.

CE entered the front room, which was burned on every wall. The ceiling, however, was only burned halfway to the front door. The bedroom off the front room had the same pattern of char on the outside wall. The wall between the front room and the bedroom was burned to a crisp, with only thin pieces of wood where a wall furnace still hung by some unknown force. The floor around the furnace was still in place. But in the corner the floor was burned through, opening a three-foot hole.

CE jumped down into the hole and looked at the underside of the floor. It was burned. He climbed out and walked around the house once more, poking into this and that before he went back to find Chief Franklin.

"It looks to me like you have a clear case of arson," CE said.

"What did you find?'

"Fire burns up, not down. The corner by the furnace is burned through, and there are char marks under the floor, as if liquid leaked through the floor before the fire started."

"That could have been the wall furnace, if it was the source, right?" asked the chief.

"Nope. The floor around the furnace is still intact. My guess right now would be that someone placed flammable liquid in front of the furnace in a container that was allowed to leak, and the liquid ran to the lowest point—the corner."

"Then who is the guy on the ground over there? And how long has he been there?"

"How long is easy. Have the lab guy cut some grass from under the body when they pick him up. I would also run his clothes for traces of liquid chemicals."

"Why the grass cuttings?"

"Photosynthesis will tell you how long the body has been there. It's like when you leave a garden hose on the grass for a long period of time and the grass underneath it turns brown. That change takes place at a given rate. So once you establish the time the body was placed there, you can compare it with the time the fire started. Now, if you don't mind, I'm going home." CE headed for his car.

"What about a game of golf this week?"

"I'll call and let you know, Chief."

CE drove home to Seal Beach in the dark. As he drove down Ocean Avenue, he noticed the streetlamp in front of his house was out. Pulling into the garage, he saw the side window open. He went to the alarm pad on the wall between the house and garage and turned off the alarm. Then he went into the house, looking around carefully for anything that seemed out of the ordinary. But everything seemed okay. He went back to the car and brought in his bag and new stamp album. As he set the bag on the floor, his eyes focused on the bookcase. He noticed that one of his albums was missing. It was his international album.

"Shit! That's my favorite album," said CE as he reached for the phone to dial the police.

The police arrived within thirty minutes, which seemed like much longer to CE, and they were as helpful as they could be on any home robbery. They came with their jargon and forms. No, they did not think fingerprints would be found, since the house was filled with natural wood furniture and that was too grainy to leave good prints of the perpetrators. No, the album most likely would not be found. They did, however, recommend that CE go around to nearby stamp dealers and check with them. The department could not spare the manpower for one stamp album. They left CE with their forms and a pit in his stomach from the feeling that they did not believe his story of being robbed. After all, the alarm did not go off, and there was no record with the company of it going off. He made a mental note to look into how easy it was to bypass alarms.

As he grieved over the lost album, he looked over the new album from Oroville. The album was the same type and style as the missing one. He opened the album to the front page and saw for the first time a handmade page with four Deutsches Reich stamps on it. Under each stamp was a German word. The top left had the word for year, top right the word for organization, bottom left the word for travel, and the word for country was on the bottom right.

"Now why the devil would someone do that?" he asked himself.

Continuing through the album, he noticed that at the end of the stamps from each country, there were a number of pages similar to the first page—but these pages had no words under the stamps. There was only a name at the top of the page, followed by a series of numbers.

"I wonder why someone would go to all the effort to make pages like this?" CE said, talking to himself again. "Well, this is a nice little mystery I can play with."

The next day, CE finished his reports and put them into the mail. He had remembered his first fire run and how the captain had

CE fill out the report. The chief told CE to place the cause of fire in the back seat of the car as "due to smoking."

"Captain, the driver does not smoke!' CE pointed out.

"Rookie," the captain replied, "some other idiot tossed the cigarette out his window, and it blew into this jerk's back seat. The wind from the open window fanned the embers. It happens all the time."

That was when CE realized that the causes of fires in many fire reports were attributed to smoking to save time. What was surprising was that cigarettes got the inflammatory reputation and not the matches. After all, cigarette burns on everything, from tables and shelves to floors and sofas, were testimonials to the fact that cigarettes were poor fire starters.

The case he had just put into the mail was a case in point. The fire had started in the master bedroom closet, and there were cigarette burns on almost every surface. The first engine company on the scene placed the origin of the fire as a cigarette. CE's report to the owner's insurance company stated that the fire started in the closet on the floor. The origin was a common white wax candle. He went on to state that the floor under the candle was not burned and that this type of candle takes forty-seven minutes to burn down—which, in CE's opinion, explained why the family was out of the house thirty minutes before the fire started.

He also made note of the fact that a high percentage of closet fires are started by children playing with matches. It was most likely not arson, since the family dog was in the house when the fire started. Family pets are removed in most attempted arsons to collect insurance. It was his professional opinion that the fire was accidental rather than intentional and that it was started by a child or children. He recommended follow-up in the area of family counseling.

The next day, CE received a call and had to make a trip back up the state. He packed his suitcase and then looked at the international album.

Why not? Maybe I can look into some of the history of this album while I'm away, he thought as he tucked the album into his suitcase.

Chapter 12

Issued January 29, 1944

Adolf Hitler was paid a royalty for every stamp with his image.

March 1945 at 3:00 a.m.—on the coast of California

The small raft slowly approached the shoreline. The man in the front, Wilhelm Steiner, began to feel the plan now had a chance of success. He thought about how his small group was destined to play a part of the greater Germanic history—a history that had always been a struggle, where great men had always stepped forward to lead Germany out of the depths of certain failure. The Fuhrer was the new and powerful destiny of the Fatherland. Steiner knew this better than any other person alive.

Wilhelm remembered the day he met the Fuhrer for the first time and was told of the plan to achieve victory for Germany. Steiner was escorted into the room, and he saw the Fuhrer standing with his hands behind his back, staring at the small group of men in the room. His eyes seemed to catch everyone at once and penetrate to the very soul of each person in the room, holding him captive. This leader was worshipped by a nation and at the same time feared by all, even those who trusted him. But fear was not his only persuasive weapon. He could also share plans and dreams in a way that those who listened to him believed everything he said was possible.

The Fuhrer stood with his most trusted party, military, industrial, and banking leaders. They all stood waiting for him to speak. When he did so, it was slow and clumsy. But then the rhythm and language image pattern of his words began to evoke their sense of national pride. He went on as if speaking to the whole nation. Most of those in the room had heard the speech many times before, but they were still caught in the illusion and magnetism of the delivery.

He spoke of the glorious history of the German people then how they suffered in order to form a great pure nation. He spoke of how Frederick the Great had faced disaster on all sides in the Seven Years War—and then, at the last moment, the nation was saved by the death of Czarina Elizabeth of Russia, which caused the new czar, Peter, to recall his troops. The victory had been made possible by Frederick's willpower. He had been willing to die and lose all to save his nation. The Fuhrer went on to say that it had always been the fate of the German people to be taken to the brink of destruction and then to be saved by the willpower of their leaders.

Now it was up to him, the Fuhrer, to bring the Reich its greatest victory. Germany was ready to turn the war back into her favor with the new secret weapons and the brave youth of the German nation. At the end of the talk, he raised his arm to return a salute and a chorus of "Heil, Hitler!" Turning, he walked into a small side room with Wilhelm, Martin Borman, and two other men, who were to be team leaders for this new special project that would save the Reich.

Each team leader was given his orders on a single piece of paper. Wilhelm looked down at the order and read the code name: Northern Wolf. His body tingled, for he knew the fate of the German New World Order and the fate of the Big Three had been set in motion in these few words.

Martin Borman then told each team leader that nothing besides this one order was to be written down and that this order was to be destroyed once the teams left German soil. Wilhelm read the rest of the orders.

Three teams, Gray Wolf, Tundra Wolf, and Timber Wolf—consisting of three agents each—will proceed to their targets and will be given all possible help without question.

—Adolf Hitler

What was not written down was that each team was made up of a group of two men and a woman, that they were all in their early twenties, except the Tundra Wolf group. They had lived most of their lives in the countries where they were being sent. Their manners and speech patterns were more like the countries where they were being sent than their homeland, Germany. They were the perfect agents—unknown.

Now, Great Britain would pay for its stubbornness after the fall of France, and the Soviet Union would be punished for its resistance to the New Order. But most of all, the Americans would now pay for their aid to the English during 1940 and 1941. The Americans were the ones who made it possible for that little island to hold out and keep the German nation from its natural place in the world order. Hitler had plans for that country filled with Indians and gangsters he learned about from the Western novel writer Carl May and Hollywood films.

America would pay for supplying Great Britain and the Soviet Union with war materials faster than the Germany army could destroy or capture them.

Hitler's vengeance against America had started as early as 1937, when he had plans to bomb the eastern coast of the US from the Azores with the Me-264, a four-engine Messerschmitt bomber, as soon as it went into full production. Yet plans had to be set aside as the war situation changed. Bomber plans were stopped because of the demand for fighter planes. So the jet bomber became a jet fighter plane, which caused more delays in production and design. Now Germany was under attack from Allied bombers, and fighters were needed to stop the night and day bombing. So, the jet fighter was being rushed to get into production.

A desperate Germany would not be upstaged any longer. Bold actions and plans would save the day. The German military had not been bold with the Americans—and that must change. And the fact that those inferior little yellow Japanese had shelled the western coastline of America early in the war in places called Seattle, Astoria, and Goleta made his anger burn hotter. His own U-boats had left the American East Coast alone, only attacking shipping lanes.

Now the Fuhrer had a plan that would change the war in his favor. But the military would not play a part because he did not trust them. This would to be a Nazi party plan backed by important financial supporters. Those generals were cowards and afraid of defeat ever since the occupation of the Rhineland by the French and Belgians in the 1920s. Furthermore, the July attempt on his life had made him distrust all but his most loyal party members. This was their plan, a gift to the future—and it was to be the fate of Germany and the world, even if he was killed. Fate had been set in motion and would determine the outcome for a greater Germany.

Chapter 13

Wehrmacht Series—issued March 21, 1943

Schnellboot S14-17

March 1945—Operation Gray Wolf

Gray Wolf's agents were to progress by U-boat to Ireland, then, with the help of the Irish Republican Army, move on to London. The IRA was being used because there was some concern about the reliability of German agents working inside England. Therefore, this operation was conducted outside the normal espionage channels. Spanish contacts were used to making arrangements with the IRA and set the operation in place.

The Gray Wolf team boarded the U-boat in Spanish waters and headed for Ireland late at night. The weather was calm, and there was no moon. The U-boat captain, knowing that these waters were no longer safe, had decided to stay submerged until he came close to land. There was no need to invite detection by Allied planes and ships.

Though the trip was short, the crew could not relax, even though this was not a combat mission. They knew the mission was important because of the two men and woman on board. It was dangerous to be in these waters. Then, as the U-boat approached the coast of Ireland, they all heard the scraping of iron on the hull. They froze and listened. Before anyone could say a word, an explosion shook the U-boat, and seawater poured into the forward compartments. The crew worked frantically to close the watertight doors. The U-boat had hit an underwater sea mine that had broken free of its anchor and drifted into the Irish Sea off the coast.

The crew rushed to the task of saving the ship and its passengers. The water poured through the hull. The only chance to save the ship was to seal the forward compartment as quickly as possible. Ship safety came first, and one crewman was sealed alive in the front compartment, drowning to save his comrades.

At that moment, an Allied plane in the area spotted the explosion and changed course to investigate. The pilot flew low and spotted the U-boat. He banked the plane to the left and climbed to line up for a bombing run. As he came back for the kill, the U-boat was close to the surface. The first bomb from the plane hit the aft torpedo room, setting off further explosions. A second bomb hit the coning tower, and water filled the U-boat and the lungs of its crew and pas-sengers. Fate had pushed Operation Gray Wolf from its important part in world history.

Chapter 14

Wehrmacht Series—issued March 21, 1943

MG-Schutzen der Waffen-SS

March 1945—Operation Tundra Wolf

Tundra Wolf's agents were sent to the Russian front. Their leader, Aleksei Dolgun, was born in Germany. At the end of the Great War, in 1920, his parents moved to the Soviet Union. His father had been a member of the German Communist Party and wanted to be in the vanguard of the new political order that was taking place in Russia. At the end of 1927, Aleksei's father was arrested as a foreign spy and sent to a gulag. He was accused of working with American and British advisors to help Russia develop industrial plants. Stalin was solidifying his hold on power and saw any contact with the West as a threat.

Aleksei's father continued to work for the state until he died five years later in Siberia.

The family left Leningrad because of their father's criminal record. The family made its way back to Germany by way of Finland after the arrest of Aleksei's father. The trip to Germany was tough and the family lost most of what they carried with them. Aleksei had a hard time fitting in with his mother's friends of the Social Democrats who Aleksei saw as nothing better than the Reds. Then, in 1931, Aleksei joined the Hitler Youth. He was going to repay the Reds and Stalin for their treatment of his father and family. In 1934 he was in the German Army when it marched across the bridge back into the Rhineland. In 1945 came orders to report to Berlin for special assignment. He was appointed to head a group of three on a special mission.

As team leader, Aleksei set about picking two other members for his team. First, there was Anna, a Russian-born German of the aristocrat society. She had been driven out of the Soviet Union during the Civil War. When communist leaders had entered her town and started the Red Terror to rid the society of counterrevolutionaries, capitalists, and spies, Anna's mother was dragged from their home and made to kneel in the street by the secret police. They asked her where the family's money and jewelry were hidden. Then two of the men went into the house to confiscate the family's valuables while another soldier stayed outside and allowed peasants to kick and beat

Anna's mother. When the two returned from the house, they laughed and called Anna's mother a capitalist whore. Then they shot her in the head.

Anna, who was ten years old at the time, had watched the whole scene from across the street with a friend of the family, who kept her from running into the street to be with her mother. In the next few days, she heard of her fathers' death while fighting the Reds. Anna was sent to Poland and then on to Germany so that her family could care for her. Anna soon joined the Hitler Youth.

The third member of the team was Ivan, the son of Russian immigrants to Finland in the 1920s. Ivan had fought against the Soviets during the Winter War. Germany had agreed to allow Stalin rights in the Baltic States in the Nonaggression Pact of 1939. Stalin saw his chance to obtain more ports in the Baltic Sea at great cost to Finland, but Finland did not prove to be an easy victory.

The Soviet Union and Germany had made a secret agreement in the early 1920s that allowed the German Army to train in secret in Russia in exchange for training the Soviet military. Then, when Stalin solidified his power, he used purges to remove opposition and keep others off balance. However, during the Great Purge, most of his officers were removed or killed. So the Winter War started with poorly led Soviet troops against the well-disciplined army of Finland.

Ivan was captured in the early days of the war, when Finland was giving the Red Army a lesson in winter warfare. The Soviets, in their paranoia, saw his name and treated him not as a prisoner of war but as a traitor. He was loaded into the lead truck in a convoy headed for Leningrad for a mock trial. The movement in the mountains was slow and dangerous in the early days of the war, and the convoy leader was nervous. When the truck hit a land mine, the commissar, fearing he was under attack, yelled for the next driver to push the disabled truck off the road. Ivan and other prisoners were tossed into a snowbank.

When Ivan regained consciousness a few minutes later, he discovered he was not alone. Two Fins, one with a broken foot, and one Soviet guard with a piece of metal in his chest were alive. Ivan and the two Fins set off with their comrade, holding the Fin broken foot between them. The Russian was left to his own fate. Two days later they rejoined the Finnish Army. They were on the front lines when Finland gave into the Soviet giant. Ivan joined the German Army right after Germany invaded Russia in 1941.

In 1945 Aleksei had worked a miracle to get the team to the eastern front. Railway, roads, and air transportation were in chaos. Trains that did move east were empty or loaded with wine from France for some imaginary victory instead of ammunition and other needed supplies. Most traffic was headed for Germany—and not always in a disciplined formation. At military checkpoints, men were pulled from the lines and papers were reviewed. Executions were done on the spot if the papers were not in order. As the Tundra team passed the retreating army, they were jeered with insults and taunts. "Say hello to Comrade Stalin. He is right behind us!"

Reaching the battlefront, Aleksei walked into the village and gave his orders to the SS commander and waited. The air was thick with snow, and Russians were hitting the Germans with shells. The shooting was getting louder and closer.

"So what do you want me to do?" asked the commander.

"I need you and your men to help us infiltrate the enemy after you leave this place."

"Just how do we do this if we are gone?"

"Easy, you will shoot each one of us. Your men are experts at pistol shooting and know where to wound people."

"My people know how to kill people and make it painful, not decorate them with gunshots."

"This mission could change the war in our favor. I have spoken personally with the Fuhrer, and that should tell you how important this mission is to Germany. Do you understand?"

The commander, duly scolded, took a more humble tone. "Yes, if you want to get shot and join the Russian Army, I will do what I can. They will be here any minute now."

The members of the team took off their heavy warm German coats. Aleksei tore up his orders and threw them into the fire. Then the team walked outside, saluted the officer with outstretched arms, and stood waiting by a pit filled with bodies.

"Right, Sergeant, let's get this done and be on our way before Ivan gets here," said the major.

An SS sergeant walked over and shot each member with a well-placed round from a pistol. The SS man smiled. He was proud of his work. The wounds looked serious, but the damage was minor, and the cold would control the bleeding.

Two SS men grabbed hold of each team member and dragged them onto the pile of bodies in the death pit behind the house. Many of the bodies were frozen and covered with snow.

As the SS men walked back into the house, someone yelled, "INCOMING!" A Russian artillery barrage began with a deafening sound. Those in the house did not hear it, but it was a direct hit, killing all inside the house.

The members of Timber Wolf lay on the pile of bodies. The bleeding had stopped almost immediately. Only the excruciating cold dulled the pains of the wounds. The artillery barrage died down, and the T-34 tanks and troops began their advance on the village. Retreating German soldiers ran past the pile of bodies.

As Russian tanks started to move into the village, the lead tank, commanded by Vladimir Kalinin, spotted movement to his left and opened fire before seeing that it was not a German tank but a pile of bodies. He immediately saw his mistake and returned to the advance. The advancing Russian troops could investigate the pile.

Aleksei had seen the Russian tanks and started waving and yelling, "Comrades! Comrades!" when the lead tank opened fire with its machine gun, cutting the team leader in half. His blood was splattered across the face of the female of the team, and she started to scream. She jumped up and ran toward the Russian infantry with a group of peasants. The peasants were shot down as traitors. The German member died with them.

The following day, a pile of frozen corpses were found in the village and photographed for the news and propaganda machine. Each corpse in the pile was frozen to the other, except for one brave lone corpse with a wound in the arm who was found a few feet away from the pile. He had crawled away from the pile in the night and was frozen where he lay. Red Army photographers took many pictures of this grizzly pile and its lone survivor, whom they reported had tried to rejoin the Red Army after the defeat of the German war machine. He was the last member of Operation Tundra Wolf and was given a Red Army hero's burial. The last member of the team had played his part in history, with an ironic twist of fate.

Chapter 15

Wehrmacht Series—Issued March 21, 1943

Fallschirmjäger

April 1945 at 3:05 a.m.—Operation Timber Wolf

The Timber Wolf team was sent to the Santa Barbara coast, off the west coast of the United States. The journey was long and dangerous. Had it been done early in the war, it would have been celebrated as a great naval victory voyage and placed in the history annals of the German Navy. A German U-boat crossing two oceans without detection by superior air and naval forces was a feat to celebrate.

Wilhelm Steiner heard the surf pounding the California shore. There were few lights on this section of isolated coast. Early in the war, the Japanese had caused a panic by attacking and shelling a nearby oil refinery. The submarine had fired a few rounds and missed everything but sand and land. Since that time, the fear of a Japanese invasion had diminished to an almost casual enforcement. Japan was on the run, losing island after island, and Germany was living in cellars in payback air raids for London.

Steiner and the small rubber boat took less than ten minutes to reach the surf. Within fifteen minutes, three figures from the U-boat had reached the road, looking like any other group of young Americans hitchhiking on Highway 101. If they were stopped by anyone, they would say that they had been out with some friends and their friends had driven off, leaving them on the desolate highway.

Wilhelm did not fear the police in America. In the late 1930s, the police had picked up a German spy on a Friday night with the blueprints marked secret—which later turned out to be plans for a newly designed bomb site. They tried to turn him over to FBI agents, but they were told that the state department was closed, so they released the German spy and told him to report back to them on Monday morning. He disappeared with the bomb-site plans and was never seen again in the United States. Germany had the bomb site while America's allies had to wait until 1941.

There also was a case early in the war on the East Coast where the FBI did arrest some real German spies, who arrived in a U-boat. But this was not because of good police work. One of the spies feared the worst and turned the other members of his team over to police in exchange for his life.

But Steiner's team was expecting better results. The plan was for them to meet their contact, a wine grower of Italian descent, on Highway 101. He would take them to the train station, where the team would board the train and cross the continent, arriving at Warm Springs, Georgia on April 9, 1945.

The war in Europe ended on May 7, 1945, and Timber Wolf's mission was lost in the victory aftermath. The team members escaped detection and resumed their American lives.

Chapter 16

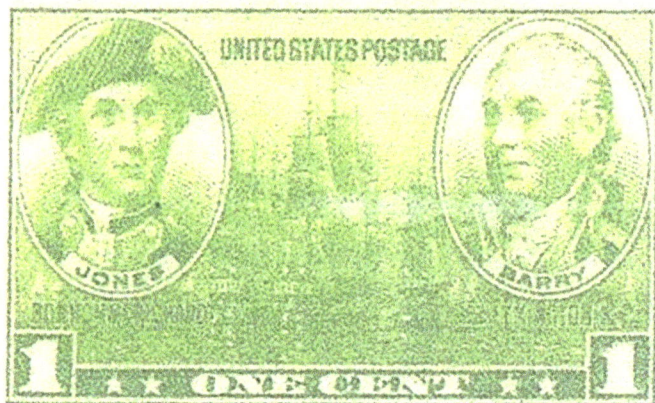

Navy (John Paul Jones and John Barry)— issued December 15, 1936

John Paul Jones defeated the HMS *Serapis* after a three-hour battle, losing his own ship, the *Bonhomme Richard*. John Barry commanded the *Lexington*, the first American ship to take a naval prize, the HMS *Edward*.

August 6, 2001—Orville, California

Back in Northern California on another industrial case, CE decided to stop by the stamp store on his way home to look into the history of his new album. Just as he pulled up in front of the store, an old man closed the door, posting a sign that said "Out of Business."

"Excuse me, sir!" CE called. "Are you the owner?"

"No, he is dead. Killed in a robbery last week!"

"I'm sorry to hear that. What happened?"

"The story is that someone killed him to get the keys to the shop. That's all I know."

"That's terrible! Crime never takes a rest!"

CE did not know why he went there; something made him go, but he ended up at the coroner's office. He found the coroner in a large rectangular room, uncomfortable in its cleanliness, with white polished floors and stainless steel tables standing in the center.

"Can I help you?" the coroner asked.

"Yes, I'm an insurance investigator, and I was wondering about the death of the coin store owner the other day." CE pulled out his identification for the coroner to inspect.

"Not much to say about it. Ed was stabbed with a knife into the heart. Whoever did it could have been a surgeon. It was done so nicely. That was a busy day. We had three bodies at once!"

"Three is a lot for a town this size! Who were they?"

"Yeah, it is, but we cover the county. Anyway, it was Ed, some other guy named Stan Larson, and an old woman who was a death camp survivor. Named Heidi Miller, I think."

Something in CE's memory started to nag in him. His mind leaped to the stamp album and the name inscribed inside: Heidi Miller. "What can you tell me about her?"

"She lived around here since the late 1940s. She stayed to herself, for the most part. She was a bit strange. My dad said she was a looker in his day. Bu, in time, she grew old and heavy, and that is what killed her. Her heart just gave out. She could cheat the Nazis but not the Grim Reaper. She had her camp number tattooed on the inside of her right arm. I can show you the pictures." He started to rummage through the desk. "See? Right there—5512306," said the coroner's tech as he pointed to the number in the photograph.

"Doc, this woman was in the camps all right, but she was on the other side of the wire."

"What do you mean?"

"Well, first of all, the Nazis did not waste time tattooing prisoners on the inner arm. They placed the tattoos on the lower arm, where it could be done fast and where it was always visible. Most important, however, is that you are reading it wrong. Look! It says SS12306, not 5512306."

"I'll be damned. You might be right! She was a Nazi!"

"Doc, I know this is unusual, but can I get a copy of the photo?"

"Take that one. I have the negative. I'll be damned—a Nazi! If that don't beat all!" He paused to think for a moment. "Well, I do not want the attention that this will generate. So as far as I'm concerned, the file will stay the way it was—finished and filed."

"I would make the change and not tell anyone," advised CE. "Just to keep the record straight."

As CE left the coroner's office, he bumped into a deputy sheriff.

"Excuse me, Deputy! I am an insurance investigator, and I am looking into the death of Heidi Miller. Do you know where I can find more information about the case?"

"Yes, I remember the old lady. Sad case—to go through what she went through and then die all alone. I was the first one to arrive on the scene."

"Did you notice anything unusual while you were there?"

"Well, I don't think there was anything suspicious about her death. But there was a spot on the bookshelf that seemed odd at the time. I was going to look for the book, but I had another call. We had three dead bodies that day, did you hear?"

"How big was the spot on the shelf that caught your attention?"

"Well, the clean area was big enough for me to notice it. I'd say maybe three or four inches wide. Why? Do you think it has something to do with her death?"

"No, the guy inside said she died of heart failure. I just like to collect all the information I can so I get to know the case. Thanks for the time and information."

"By the way, her landlord, the guy who called in the death, fell down his steps that night and died."

"Was it an accident?"

"That's what it looked like and the coroner ruled it an accident. Why are you asking?"

"Just that when three people die the same day and two of them are connected, it just seems a little strange. Don't you think?"

"Yeah, but there did not seem to be another connections and the coroner ruled one accidental."

CE headed toward his car. But his mind was far away. *It is strange that three people died on the same day. And it's even more strange that they were all connected somehow. Yet, it was a small town...*

Miller 5512306

Chapter 17

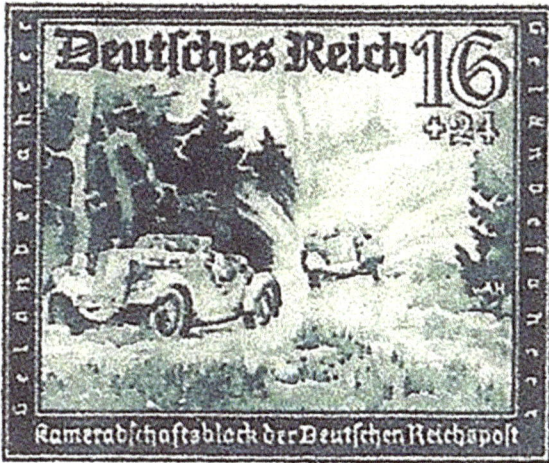

Gelandefahren—issued September 15, 1939

January 1945, Germany—Heidi Miller

Heidi Miller was born in Germantown, Pennsylvania to a family that came to the United States in 1922. Heidi was born one month after getting off the boat. She grew up healthy, like most young Americans at the time, and she was quick with numbers and organization. In 1933, when Heidi was eleven, her family moved back to Germany. Her father had joined the Nazi Party, and Heidi became a member of the Hitler Youth at the age of twelve. The family encouraged this, since it would help her father's position in the local party structure. Heidi's mother saw it as a wonderful way for Heidi to become a good German and rid herself of those awful American habits. The Americans had too much freedom, and that was bad for young people. The Hitler Youth would reestablish order with marching, singing, and outdoor activities. Local party leaders would give speeches about German values and German motherhood. This would straighten out any of Heidi's confused ideas.

Motherhood in Germany was raised to the level of a national honor. Mothers with large families were given medals by the Fuhrer and placed in positions of honor in the community.

The youth movement looked wonderful on the outside. But inside, the movement was quite different. Germany needed to rebuild its war machine, and it needed men. Heidi enjoyed the marching and camping and considered it great fun.

One night, the girls were encouraged to help the Fatherland rebuild its manpower. Young women were not forced physically into sexual relationships with male members, but the needs of the country and peer pressure found Heidi in love and pregnant in 1939. The father of the child was an SS man who had been killed in a training accident in July of that year. They were to have been married in August.

Heidi's son was born with a deformity and died within minutes. The doctors in the SS hospital said his lungs were filled with fluids and he never took a breath, but they had allowed him to die. New Germany did not need cripples and deformed men. These doctors were part of the euthanasia program to help Germany rid itself of the "useless eaters"—those individuals who were unworthy of living in the New Reich. Individuals with deformities and incurable medical problems were selected for mercy killings with lethal injections in the T-4 Program. The program was stopped when the public started to hear the rumors. The doctors and technicians later became part of the Final Solution 1941.

Heidi never overcame her grief and withdrew into her own mind. She rarely talked to anyone and had no friends. Her parents pushed her to join the army to get her life in order and to get her out of the house. A party member did not need a "weak-headed" daughter.

Then, in 1941, Heidi volunteered for the SS and was immediately selected for service.

With her blonde hair, blue eyes, and picturesque German face, she was the perfect German woman. She was given a nurse's uniform and shown how to inject medicine. Then she was sent to Poland to work in a Jewish resettlement camp.

At the camp, Heidi performed her job with such efficiency that the medical ward almost looked like a real hospital. The doctors were amazed at how patients allowed Heidi to inject them with death and still smile up at her, as though they were looking into the eyes of an angel. But though she was beautiful on the outside, Heidi showed no emotion.

In January of 1945, a young officer named Wilhem Steiner came to the camp and asked Heidi to go to America on a special mission. Steiner had read her file and was amazed at how perfect she was for the mission—a nurse and a whiz with numbers and records. She was perfect!

Steiner observed her at work at the medical ward. At each bed, she would talk to the patient and take his temperature with a thermometer while stroking his forehead or arm, speaking in a low soothing voice. Then she would read the thermometer and make a note of the temperature on the medical chart.

Next, she would pick up a syringe, swab the patient's arm with water, and inject the death serum into the patient's arm without a word. Steiner could not forget one Jewish girl with green eyes. As

Heidi went through her routine, the young girl kept lovingly patting Heidi's hand until her life was gone.

Heidi accepted the offer to join the team and found herself riding a train across America in 1945. She loved to ride trains. She would close her eyes and sway with the cars as she listened to the sound of the wheels on the rails. In fact, train rides were the only thing Heidi enjoyed outside of her stamp collection and its secrets.

Chapter 18

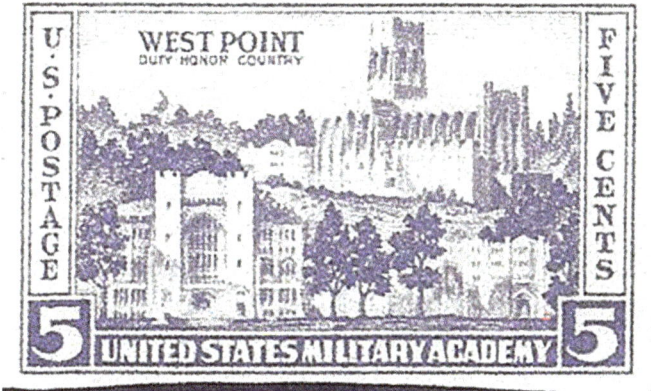

**Army Military Academy at West Point,
New York—issued May 26, 1937**

Established by Congress in the Academy in 1802, the academy sits on the Hudson River and can control the river traffic. Benedict Arnold tried to turn the fortress over to the British, and he was stopped at the last minute before he escaped to a British warship. The British officer that worked with Arnold was captured and hung as a spy.

March 1945—Santa Barbara, California

Vitto Carbo was waiting for his passengers on the shoulder of Pacific Coast Highway, just outside of Santa Barbara. He had been told to wait no more than thirty minutes and to act as if he were fixing a flat tire. If his passengers did not show up, he was to return at the same time for the next five nights. The contact that gave him the information was a Swiss associate with a banking firm that Vitto did overseas business with at times.

This part of the highway was desolate, dark, and lonely, with only the sound of waves hitting the beach just on the other side of the railroad tracks. The night sky was filled with the stars, but it was dark, as the moon was not visible.

Vitto had his reasons for what he was doing. Some people might call it treason, but that did not bother him. He was comfortable with his actions. He sat on the side of the road with his sleeves rolled up and the car jack at his side, looking around for his German passengers. Three years ago, the West Coast was in a panic of a Japanese attack. Now there was no fear of an invasion. The Japanese on the West Coast had been rounded up and sent to camps, and some German and Italians were also sent to camps. Vitto was looking to the future and how to control the liberal Left.

Chapter 19

United States Naval Academy at Annapolis, Maryland—issued May 26, 1937

Franklin Delano Roosevelt announced at a press conference on March 7, 1936 that he had requested the Post Office Department to issue a series of stamps to honor military and naval heroes. Congress established the Academy in 1845.

May 1915—San Francisco, California

Vitto had arrived in America in May of 1915, when he jumped ship from his Italian merchant marine vessel in the port of San Francisco to escape the war in Europe. He was not a coward, and war did not scare him. He just wanted to choose for himself. He did not want to be at the whim of some political leader who did not even know his name.

Vitto had plans, yet these had been interrupted when he had robbed a minor Mafia boss and slept with that same man's young wife. She had saved herself by screaming rape when the husband walked into the house. Wasting no time with dressing, Vitto grabbed his pants, jumped out the second-story window, and ran down the alley before the husband was able to run up the stairs to catch him. The young wife played the performance of a hysterical victim for the next week. Vitto knew the time was right to move on. He did not stop running until he reached the docks and was hired on a merchant ship that left port that same night.

Vitto's life in San Francisco had been fun and carefree. To make money, he and his girlfriend, Beth, had lured drunken seamen up to her apartment and robbed them when their pants were down. They made a good living until one night, when one of the suckers was not so drunk and started to feel uneasy.

"What are you waiting for? Most women I pick up are in bed before I get my pants down."

"I like to watch and see what I'm going to be getting."

"That's crap! You're a whore, and you will not remember my name, let alone part of my body. Now what is your game, sweetheart?" the sailor asked in a menacing voice.

Beth, realizing this could get out of hand, placed her hands on her hips and said, "You're drunk and insulting! Get out!"

"The hell I will! I came here for some fun, and you are going to show me some fun one way or another!" He raised his arm and stepped closer to Beth.

Beth's defiant stand melted into fear as the man's hand slapped her face. She yelled, "You drunken bastard! You'll pay for that!" He responded by punching Beth in the face, breaking her nose and sending her to the floor.

Vitto jumped out of the closet and confronted the man. He yelled as the man picked up a chair and raised it over his head. "You want to play? Then come on then, let's play. I'll beat the crap out of you and that bitch of yours!"

Vitto ducked under the chair as it swung past his head. He jumped at the seaman, hitting him just below the chest, which sent the man falling backward. The sailor went through the open part of the window and crashed to the street below.

Vitto did not waste a minute. He took off for the farm country, leaving Beth to explain how a naked man jumped out her window and how she had broken her nose. Vitto knew he would be invisible once he joined the migrant workers.

In the wine country, Vitto worked at different ranches and vineyards until in 1921, when his life took a sudden change for the better. Vitto was working at Victor McDonnel's ranch for about a week when Mr. McDonnel sent Vitto to the house to refill the lemonade jug. Mr. McDonnel was the son of a Scottish immigrant who married the daughter of an old California Spanish family.

The ranch raised cattle for their hides, called California dollars by many because leather could be used for many applications. In the 1880s, McDonnel's father switched from cattle to citrus trees and grapes just before the cattle market collapsed.

Vitto stood just under six feet tall and had that handsome Valentino dark Mediterranean look. He was strong and worked hard when the situation required it. He was not lazy, but he took any opportunity that came his way—and that day it was Hannah McDonnel.

Hannah McDonnel was a headstrong tall handsome woman. She had seen Vitto twice before she found him walking up the path from the field. The first time she saw him was when he beat another farmhand senseless over a debt. Her father had told the loser to get off the property—not for losing the fight but for not paying his debts. The second time was when she watched Vitto outtrade a man in a deal, leaving the other guy to believe that he had taken Vitto for his last dollar.

Today's meeting was a turning point for the two of them. Vitto walked into the kitchen with his mind on quick romance. What he did not know was that Hannah was a better negotiator than he was.

"Your father sent me to get some more lemonade."

"He should not be working out in that heat," Hannah said.

"I'll try to get him to sit in the shade when I get back…if you want me to."

"Yes, that would be nice, if you could." She paused in a calculated fashion. "He will not take orders. He has his pride."

"I'll tell him that the shade has a gentle breeze that will brush his face like a soft kiss and that is how the owner of the land should enjoy the pleasures of his land always."

"You are a clever fellow with a tongue of a poet. What is your name?" she asked, already knowing it.

"Vitto Carbo," he said.

Their courtship started that day, and they were married in 1922 at a large wedding in the orange grove. The wedding was wonderful and grand. They stayed at home to honeymoon so that they could help her father with the ranch.

That night she had come to him wearing only her wedding veil, and they fell into bed. He had taken her to the point of pleasurable pain, and it had given him the feeling of total control to hear her little cries of joy with each peak. However, for Vitto it was a Pyrrhic victory he had not controlled that moment. Hannah allowed herself to enjoy the satisfaction with complete abandonment, knowing she controlled the relationship.

Two days after the wedding night, in an argument over some small thing, Vitto slapped Hannah and told her to shut up. She said nothing to him, but she looked him straight in the eyes and went back to work in the kitchen. After the dinner dishes were done, they went to bed and made love. Later that night, when the room was dark and Vitto's mind slipped into a peaceful sleep, he dreamed of vines brushing his face and neck as he heard Hannah's voice softly talking to him.

"Look at me, Vitto!" Vitto started to open his eyes slowly with pleasure, until he realized that the vines of his dream were in fact a sharp metal knife pressed on his neck. His eyes popped open wide to see Hannah's calm, lovely, menacing eyes.

"What is it?" he choked out.

"Move, my dear husband, and you may never move again. Just lie there and listen. I, Hannah Carbo, do not like being hit and will not be hit again! Do you understand that?"

Vitto stared up at her and said nothing.

"Tell me you understand."

He nodded his head and felt the edge of the knife nick the outer layer of skin. He could feel warm blood on his neck. It was the first time in Vitto's life he was afraid.

"I want to hear your words, my dear," she said as she pressed the blade a little harder into his neck.

"Yes, I understand! I understand!" came weakly from his lips.

"If you ever hit me again, I will take this butcher knife and cut off your private parts and stuff them into your mouth just before I slit your throat as you sleep! You will never be safe, but there is no reason to live in fear! I love you. Do you understand me, my husband?" The words were not said in rage—just a cold, calm, simple statement of fact. Then she pressed the knife closer to his throat a little deeper.

"Yes!"

Panic was in his eyes before she released the pressure and said, "Now, will you have some coffee before going to the fields?" she said in her loving voice.

Speechless, he nodded. Vitto began to realize he had married better than he knew. She was the real partner he needed, and she saw the world as he did—something to be controlled and taken. Vitto never hit his wife again.

They had their first son in 1923, and they named him Victor, for Hannah's father. A second son, Gino, came in 1924, the year Hannah's father died. Hannah and Vitto inherited the ranch and started to build an empire after a proper mourning period.

In 1925, Vitto started to bootleg wine for San Francisco's elite, which included government officials from the state and city governments. That same year, a San Francisco bootlegger arrived at the ranch with his girlfriend, whose name just happened to be Beth. They drove into the yard, where Vitto was digging.

"Hi, Vitto" called Beth.

"I'll be damned! How is it you found me?" Vitto asked.

"I saw you deliver a load of wine to the place I sometimes work at," Beth said.

"Yeah!" the bootlegger said. "We figured you were doing pretty good and could share with us since you left poor little Beth here holding the bag a few years back. That situation would make a good story for the right people, don't you think?"

Vitto looked at the little worm and smiled. "Yeah, but who is to say that good old Beth here hasn't told half the city since then?"

"I am no rat, Vitto! I did not tell a single soul until I saw you deliver that load the other day! Then I told Harry here the story."

"That's right," Harry said, "and I said to her, 'Let's get into the car and get ourselves cut into some of your old boyfriend's action! After all, she has your balls in her hands, and she'll do what I tell her to do!" Then he started to pull out his gun.

Vitto threw the shovel blade first into the man's neck, causing him to jerk to the left as he pulled the trigger. Beth froze as the bullet entered her left eye. She fell dead next to the bootlegger, who was choking to death on his own blood.

Vitto packed the two of them neatly into their car and drove it into the hole for his new barn, which doubled as a wine cellar. He poured the concrete floor over their car, sealing them inside.

Vitto's business flourished until 1926, when farm prices started a downward spiral. Vitto suspected that the socialists in California would try to control his property, so Vitto became a financial supporter of Mussolini. When the Great Depression started and FDR's New Deal threatened the free market, Vitto became even more involved with fascist businessmen.

However, he remained outside the party to stay above suspicion. This allowed him to use his influence in the community to the benefit of his Italian friends.

Hannah's father had been a tight-fisted man, with a grip on every penny. He was never one to waste anything. He would rather leave the dinner table hungry than to have leftovers. So when Vitto inherited that tidy sum of money and the ranch, he started to build an empire.

Vitto bought the small farms around his ranch when his neighbors could not pay their debts. He then expanded his crops to include olives. By 1938, McDonnel Ranch was one of the largest in the state, producing wine for both the best tables and paper-bag drinkers in America.

Vitto knew money greased the machinery of bureaucratic red tape, so he gave funds to both political parties. His contributions were small at first and then larger as benefits increased. Local governments were easier to manipulate, as there were fewer people to deal with and results came cheaper. Local corruption did not think big.

Vitto had local officials change one word here and there in the local building codes and saved more money than he ever gave to local political parties. When Prohibition ended, he had his storage buildings classified as agricultural buildings to lower his building permit costs. His wine pressing became an agriculture process rather than a business operation. One word in the law could make or break an industry's profit, and money to the right party could have a word added or deleted. Vitto had become a major player in the power game.

Chapter 20

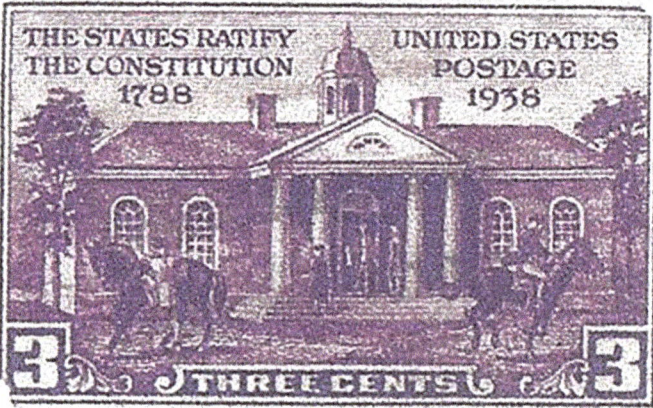

Constitution Ratification—issued June 21, 1938

FDR selected this design for the 150th anniversary of the ratification of the United States Constitution. Nine States had ratified the constitution by June 21, 1788, but it was not until 1790 that ratification was completed. Congress went through over 145 proposed amendments before adding ten to the Constitution.

March 1945—Pacific Coast Highway

Vitto sat with the tire jack by his side. His mind wandered to the many ways the war had added to his wealth. It was wealth more than anything that allowed him to keep his sons from being called up in the draft. Wealth and the war had allowed him to place each son on important war industry boards, making the family influence wider and preparing the family for the industrial cutbacks that were inevitable at the end of the war. As a precaution, he had given each son enough land and livestock to qualify for an agriculture deferment from the draft board.

A sound made him look toward the railroad tracks. He saw three people stepping across the tracks as if they had just stopped to see the surf.

"How was the water?" Vitto called out, waiting for the correct response.

"Perfect for the feet," the tallest of the trio said, striding toward the car.

"We better get going, or you will miss your train," Vitto said with a nod as he started the engine. The three strangers got into the car, and the group drove off in silence.

"In the envelop in the glove compartment are your train tickets and some cash. There are some newspapers in the back there. One is local news and the other a national paper that will give you the latest news so you will be up to date on what is happening," said Vitto.

"Thank you, that will help us catch up on current events in the states," said the tall man.

Vitto looked at the man and woman in the back seat. She was beautiful, but there was something about her eyes—vacant. The man next to her was well dressed and still had that look Vitto was all too familiar with since his days in San Francisco. The tall man in the front seat was everything a businessman should be—self-assured and confident. Vitto did not know why they were here and did not care as long as it helped stop the liberal communist.

At the train station Vitto did not get out of the car. The three passengers got out and walked to the station platform to wait for the train as Vitto drove off.

Chapter 21

Briefzusteller—issued May 1944

April 1945—on the Southern Pacific Railroad

The dining car was a busy place during serving time, as waiters moved up and down the aisles at the beckoning of seated diners. The line of those waiting to be seated stretched beyond the dining car into the adjoining coach car. The train rocked back and forth with the steady rhythmic motion as wheels rolled across gaps in the rails, creating an almost hypnotic sound. For some, standing in line broke the boredom of waiting in a cramped seat, where sleep was hard to come by. For others, standing in line was an opportunity to talk with others and overcome the isolation created by the social conventions of public transportation. For still others, impatience was the only thought as they shuffled from one foot to another waiting to be served.

Uniformed military personnel filled the majority of the train's seats, which meant the military police occasionally passed through the cars, reprimanding those who were loud or drunk. The conductor systematically moved through the cars checking tickets. Not once did Steiner see passengers being asked for passports or identification papers. *There is no order here,* Steiner thought as the MPs slowly made their way through the dining car. *What they need is the Gestapo.*

Steiner and Heidi sat in the dining car across from a mature couple, who introduced themselves as Herbert and Margaret Love. They were professors at a small private college in western New York, and they were returning from a lecture tour in California. It was apparent from their conversation that they had spent every moment in their sleeper car planning every single detail of their trip, down to the moment that they would arrive in the dining car. They were very patient and polite to the waiters and seemed to enjoy every mundane second of the dining experience. Steiner subconsciously stared across the table, watching Herbert appear to be engrossed as Margaret reminisced over what they had for lunch.

"We had that wonderful roasted chicken with walnut and maple glaze at lunch, so let's try the red meat tonight." She looked at Steiner and Heidi as if they should agree and then continued the conversation without hesitation. "The chicken just melted in your mouth.

There was just a hint of garlic in the olive oil and a touch of thyme to the meat. It was just delicious."

Steiner did not know how to respond to this blabbing female fool, so he just moved his head in agreement, smiling as he said, "That sounds nice."

Herbert gazed into space with his eyes closed, as though trying to visualize the perfect meal. "Why don't we try the fresh ham with roasted red cabbage and apples? It has an apple cider sauce that sounds mouthwatering." He did not open his eyes, assuming his wife was listening, which she was.

"Yes, yes, fresh ham with red cabbage and apples. Good! But we better not have the apple pie for dessert." Margaret turned to Steiner and said, "Last night we had a wonderful baked chicken with the most delicious white sauce. The carrots were cooked in butter and simply melted in your mouth. But the best was the dessert…angel food cake with sour cherry ice cream and chocolate sauce."

"Then that is settled. Shall we order the roasted ham, my dear?" asked Herbert.

"Oh, yes, yes, roast ham, and we will have the Indian pudding with butterscotch sauce for dessert. Remember the last time we had Indian pudding…" Herbert looked up into the empty space and tried to visualize the Indian pudding as his wife spoke on.

Steiner looked at these two idiots and wondered how this country could ever hope to build an army to conquer the world. With so many more important things to consider, these two spent half their time trying to figure out what they are going to eat and the rest of their time discussing what they had already eaten. "God, what a waste!" Steiner mumbled to himself as the Loves' conversation continued.

Heidi had been looking out the window, completely removed from the table conversation. In fact, she seemed so absorbed in her own thoughts that Steiner hesitated to disturb her to order dinner. She watched as the train moved through the mountains, following a river brimming with the runoff of the melting snow and across the vast rolling Great Plains. Once in a while, she would call Steiner's attention to something out the window without actually taking her eyes off of the scenery.

Steiner ate his meal and tried to ignore the droning chatter of the Loves, periodically looking out the window to avoid engaging in conversation. As the train passed through small towns, he noted that they were filled with cars and trucks moving about in every direction and wondered at the waste of fuel. In Germany, you would only see this many vehicles in a military convoy. At one station, he watched in surprise as Germany prisoners of war were loaded into trucks to be taken back to their camp after spending a day working in the rail yard and marveled that a country so soft on prisoners could possibly ever expect to win a war.

Steiner let his mind wander into the mission and how the world seemed to be linked by parallel powers. Franklin Delano Roosevelt had been sworn in as the president of the United States in 1933, the same year Adolf Hitler came to power in Germany. Both men were popular and used the mass media of radio and motion pictures to promote their views. But the differences between them were stark.

FDR was a man of wealth who tried to give the impression that he was every man—friendly, relaxed, and genuine. His "fireside chats" were broadcast on the radio, allowing him to step into the living room of every American to push his unprofitable social reforms. All but confined to a wheelchair because of a bout with polio in 1921, FDR became a symbol of American resilience. "We have nothing to fear…" he said. *Nothing to fear but weakness,* Steiner thought.

Adolf Hitler, on the other hand, used the media to demonstrate his strength as Germany's "overma." He removed his opposition inside and outside of Germany through the military force of the Sturmabteilung (Strom Detachment SA). He even ordered the murder of an entire leadership of a revolutionary group in the SA with the help of the Wehrmacht (German Army) in one the Knight of the Long Knives.

He used propaganda on radio to build his power by making radios cheap enough for everyone to afford but low-quality enough that they couldn't pick up foreign broadcasts that might challenge the German way of thinking. Rudolf Hess once said, "Adolf Hitler is Germany, Germany is Adolf Hitler." He, too, used art to influence his people. When *Triumph of the Will* was shown around the world, moviegoers were amazed at the health and strength of the German people as the rest of the world struggled through the Great Depression.

It was Hitler's strength and total control Steiner admired and what he believed the Americans feared. Radical wings of American society were beginning to see the value of a strong leader to fight back against communism, and the propaganda FDR's lackey pushed through art, films, and music to an unsuspecting public left a bitter taste in Steiner's mouth. He even collected stamps. *What a waste,* Steiner thought.

Steiner's thoughts were interrupted as the waiter served the food. The meal was peppered with constant utterances—"mmmm…" and words such as "Delicious!" and "Delightful!" followed nearly every bite. Margaret maintained a nearly unending narration of how each part of the meal was prepared and cooked.

"This sauce is delightful!" Harry said with glee.

"Let me taste yours! Mine is so wonderful. It adds to the taste of everything."

"Mmmm, so good! I hate to lose even one little taste of it! And anyway, you have the same thing."

"Oh! Stop it, Harry, let me have a taste!"

Steiner looked at Heidi and felt sadness for such a beautiful woman to be so empty and lost in a world of her own. He knew her story and for some reason had a connection to her. He would protect Heidi from more hurt.

Chapter 22

Pony Express—issued April 3, 1940

FDR approved the design and as soon as it went into circulation. Horse breeders, jockeys, and other horse people said the horse could not possibly run in the position that was depicted. Collectors rushed to buy the stamps, believing the stamp would be recalled, but instead the post office issued the Pan American stamp on April 14, 1940 to control the controversy, and the Pony Express stamp became a rarity.

August 7, 2001, at 10:05 p.m.—Interstate 5

CE hated to fly because of the confined space and lack of free movement. So he found himself on the roads of California more than most people and at times when most people were at home. He tried to miss the congested morning and evening traffic of major metropolitan areas, usually opting for early mornings or late evenings.

Tonight was no exception. He was heading south on Interstate 5, and the light traffic, made up mostly of large trucks, was moving fast. Interstate 5 had been built parallel to Highway 99, which had become more urban and congested over time, resulting in delays for the long-haul truckers. So pressure was placed on the government to build Interstate 5.

The new route cut along the eastern base of the Coastal Range foothills and away from any communities that would slow the travel time. The scenery along the interstate was open land and agricultural fields, with an occasional small town, gas station, fast-food restaurant, or rest area, interrupting the monotony.

The interstate itself was made of two long ribbons of asphalt and concrete that marked the territory claimed from nature. Each ribbon of asphalt had two lanes, with the western lanes moving in a southern direction and the eastern lanes moving traffic north. The roadbed had been cut and filled to make a flat drive across the gullies and ridges of the land, often giving the impression of driving into canyons one moment and then over ravines the next. At other times, the long stretch of foothills and the vast skyline spread out into a picturesque view of California's productive farmland, kept fertile by the California aqueduct.

On this night, a cool wind was blowing east down the hills. CE could feel it gently pushing his SUV each time it emerged out of one of the man-made canyons into the plains. Looking to his left, he could see the northbound lanes illuminated by headlights.

The ravines on this stretch could cause problems for high-profile trucks and RVs. The wind would rush up and down the ravines and hit the vehicles at a ninety-degree angle as the vehicles emerged from the protection of the grooved roadbed. The crosswind had caused many drivers to overcompensate and lose control of their vehicles.

As CE drove south with the window down, the fresh smell of the night air filled his nostrils, as if the earth were relaxing after a long hot day. He stayed in the left lane to keep the ride smooth, because the wear and tear of the big sixteen-wheelers had made the right lane bumpy.

He only moved over when he saw the headlights of another car creeping up behind him.

A dark-green Jaguar closed the gap behind CE to a distance of two or three car lengths, so CE pulled into the right lane to let the car pass. In front of CE was a big-rig truck, which was picking up speed to gain momentum for the next incline, causing it to gain on the RV that had already started up the incline.

Bob and Hazel Culp were on their first trip to the southwest in their new Pierce Arrow RV. It was a color-coordinated, streamlined home on wheels with the family runabout car towed behind. Bob's forty-year career as a midlevel manager at an educational textbook firm gave him a very optimistic view of retirement. Laws were constantly changing, and textbooks were required to adjust to the new guidelines, so Bob had learned to adjust easily. Retirement and the road trips were more predictable, and it was now within his power to control what came next. Bob never went over the speed limit, no matter how many trucks and cars honked their horns and how many drivers waved their fists and fingers at him. He was in control.

Bob's wife, Hazel, was constantly puttering around in the back of the RV, rearranging knickknacks and fixing snacks. They had stopped in Sacramento's Old Town and stayed longer than they had planned, so Bob was off his schedule and was in a hurry to make up the lost time. In his hurry, Bob had taken a shortcut when he set the locking pin that held the bolt into the latching device. He had done this many times before and had never had a problem because he drove slow and did not change lanes quickly or often.

Ralph Nelson, driving the big rig behind the RV, grumbled because the RV was not moving with the flow of traffic. Ralph was tired and had his favorite country radio station on to an old Hank

Williams song, hoping to keep himself awake. He was trying to decide whether to get off at Harrison's Ranch or go on to the next rest area.

Ralph had been driving for forty years and had seen many changes in that time. The equipment was better, and the drivers were more aggressive and less courteous to cars. But the same could be said of other drivers—like the RV driver in front of him, who was oblivious of his impact on the traffic. Big-rig trucks were forced to cut into the fast lane to pass these slower vehicles, slowing the traffic in that lane and causing a stream of cars to pile up behind them.

Halfway up the incline, Ralph pulled his truck into the left lane to maintain speed and pass the slower RV. Just then, the green Jaguar accelerated to pass an SUV, and the big rig then at the last minute darted into the left lane in front of the truck. The unexpected lane change caused the truck to back off the gas, slowing all of the traffic and creating a procession of slowly moving vehicles.

CE's SUV was now caught between the large RV and the trailer truck, forcing him to move as far to the left shoulder as possible. At that moment, the small vehicle being towed behind the RV broke free and headed in CE's direction. Luck was all that saved C.E. from going over the side and tumbling down the hill to join the northbound traffic. Just as the small vehicle and towing trailer were about to hit CE, he saw an opening in the center divider that had been made for highway patrol vehicles to turn around. CE cut the wheel to the left and exited the road on a level section, sending dust flying as he headed down the gradual slope toward the northbound traffic. After a few bumps and what seemed like an eternity with his brake pedal pushed all the way to the floor, CE came to a stop and closed his eyes.

CE sat in the vehicle for some time until he noticed that the air had a new smell. It was the cattle feed lots of Harrison's Ranch. He was alive, and the smell of cattle had never been so wonderful! He breathed deeply as the truck and RV drivers came running to see if he needed help.

"Are you okay?" they both said, almost in unison. CE nodded and looked toward the road, where traffic was already slowing to see what had happened. It took about an hour for the drivers to give their statements to the highway patrol officer who pulled up minutes later. But though all the drivers shared similar details about the incident, none of them could give a good description of the people in the Jaguar or its license plate number.

Chapter 23

**Mesa Verde National Park (un-gummed)—
issued March 15, 1935**

Postmaster General Farley had given proof sheets of several stamps to the president and other individuals as collector pieces with the stipulation that they were not to be sold. When one of these sheets turned up on the market as collateral for a loan, collectors demanded an investigation, and Congress held hearings. Reprints were sold, and the government made 1.5 million dollars in profit. The stamps are known as Farley's Follies.

August 6, 2000—Congressman Robert T. Chase's California Office

The congressman glared at the two men before him and said in a menacing tone, "WHERE IS THE ALBUM?" They stared blankly back at him. Regaining his composure, the congressman asked again, "Where is the album you were sent to get?"

"We just gave it to you," the taller of the two men said.

"This is AN album! But did you look to see if it was the right one? You were told the name in the album would be Heidi Miller with records of movement and locations! So tell me…where is the RIGHT ALBUM?"

"If that's not the right one, then we don't know," the smaller man offered. He began to feel that sinking feeling that someone was going to have to pay big for this screwup, and he didn't want it to be him. He tried to keep his knees loose so they would not start to shake and show the fear that was beginning to grow in his body. Gene Ackerman was not a man who feared physical danger. His fear came from the power of an office or position. Those situations could not be won. His fear continued to grow, almost to the level where he couldn't hear the congressman's question.

"Tell me everything that happened…I mean everything exactly as it happened," the congressmen said with a steely voice.

"We went to Heidi's house and saw the landlord, cop, and coroner. When they left, we went in and searched the place. There was nothing there except a spot in the bookshelf with no dust. I thought the landlord took the book, and I was right. We went to his house to get the book. After a little persuasion, he told us he sold the book to the coin shop in town. Then we went to the coin shop, and it was closed. So we went to his home and waited for him to take us back to the store. He started to get upset and question us a little too loud. So he was shut up andwe took the keys.

"At the store we made it look like a robbery and did not find the book, but we found a check with a name and address. We then went to that address and found that book. So if that is not the right book, I do not know where the right one is."

After the two men recounted their story, the congressman looked at them shaking his head. "You two go and find that book now!"

"Where?"

"Start at the beginning and find the book!"

They left the room and hustled quickly down the hallway, trying to put distance between themselves and the angry congressman. They did not hear him place a call to William Steiner and set up a meeting for the next day. After the call, he sat there thinking how to put distance between himself and this situation. He could not think of one. The book had to be found.

Chapter 24

**Constitution Sesquicentennial—
issued September 17, 1937**

The painting used for this stamp's design was believed to be part of the collection of the National Gallery, so permission was not sought for its replication. When it was discovered that the painting was in fact privately owned by Clarence Dillon, he gave his enthusiastic consent to use the image for the stamp.

August 9, 2001—a mountain cabin in Big Bear

William Steiner arrived at the cabin early. The mountains reminded him of life in the old country, so he always enjoyed his time there. He had been lucky enough to once visit Hitler's mountaintop retreat at Berchtesgaden in the Bavarian mountains near Salzburg. "The Eagle's Nest," as it was called, and some believed it was a present for Hitler's fiftieth birthday in 1939.

That visit was intimidating by it sheer nature. He walked first through a marble-lined tunnel some four hundred feet long guarded by SS men. At the end of the tunnel, he boarded an elevator trimmed with brass, mirrors, and green leather that took him four hundred feet up to the Kehlsteinhaus, where he stood next to a red marble fireplace that had been given to Hitler by Mussolini for the reception room and looked out the huge window at a magnificent view of the valley.

Now Steiner enjoyed a similar view of mountains and valley through the large picture window of the cabin. Though the building's design was more like a Frank Lloyd Wright than the chalet-style of the Eagle's Nest, Steiner loved it and had given this cabin a similar name: Condor's Perch.

He seated himself in a green stuffed chair as he looked out at the landscape and briefly thought that though things had changed, they never really changed. It was ironic that some fifty years later, Steiner was again enjoying the lifestyle of a man of promise. All those many years ago, the Führer had sent him on a mission to end the war in Germany's favor, but all that came falling down around him. Yet here he was, sitting in a chair with a different valley lying before him, and it was a magnificent relaxing view. He closed his eyes and drifted into the past.

Hitler's problem was he was loyal and was betrayed by those he trusted. Rudolf Hess had flown to Scotland on a stupid mission; Hermann Goring, the drug addict, and Heinrich Himmler both fled to the western allies at the end. Only the fanatical Goebbels stayed to the end with their leader. Thank God the organization is not built around an individual today.

Steiner

Chapter 25

**Wehrmacht Series: Fallschirmjager—
issued March 21, 1943**

January 1919—Germany

Fritz Steiner, William's father, had claimed to be a small-town banker in western Germany before the Great War. In reality, he had been a small-time loan shark with a talent for dealing with tough debt collections. His talents were at times noticed and used by the local bankers to encourage delinquent clients to pay their debts.

During the Great War, he had been assigned to the supply service and was able to make friends with industrial suppliers. They entered a small profit situation of kickbacks and black market deals that benefited Steiner and his old and new pals. His ability to slip from the shadow world into respectable business gave his industrialist and banker friends a resource they could use in the uncertain times that lay ahead.

The collapse of the German Empire shocked the financial community and the economy in part because of the Allied blockade that lasted until June 1919.

During that time, food was rationed to extreme levels, setting the stage for the Bavarian Red Republic revolution of 1919, which struck terror in the hearts of banking and industry magnates.

These industrialists and financiers responded by supporting ultranationalist, radically racist, virulently anti-Semitic, hysterically anti-Communist, antidemocratic authoritarian groups. Funds were channeled through Fritz to the Freikorps units, paramilitary groups that functioned as private armies for political and economic purposes. The government enlisted these right-wing groups to crush the revolutionaries. Fritz's personal stock went up, and he moved into the legitimate banking world.

At that time, Germany was a defeated nation that could not come to terms with its defeat. The fact that no armies had invaded the German national territory and the army was still holding the line helped feed the lie that the Communist and Jewish "criminals" on the home front signed the armistice in November of 1918. A year later, the British still had their blockade in place, causing the German people great suffering until they signed the Treaty of Versailles, which Fritz and his fellow Germans called the *dikat*.

Later, resentment over the treaty's forced reparations was fueled by the occupation of the Rhur by French and Belgian troops. When German workers refused to work for the French, the French imposed a curfew, withheld postal privileges, disconnected telephones, exercised censorship, mandated compulsory registration, and required identification numbers and passes to leave or enter the area. However, the most humiliating thing was that German citizens had to tip their hats to French and Belgium soldiers. The frustration caused by these restrictions allowed Fritz to collect payments from both German and Allied debtors who were unable to pay because of the strike. The Weimar government used inflation to pay the foreign debt, and this hurt the working and lower-class Germans.

Fritz developed a system of intimidation using thugs to do his dirty work. All he had to do was get a list of family and friends of the debtor and send his thugs to find out who in the family had the money to pay. His commission sometimes equaled half the debt owed to his financier friends. The underworld and business world worked together without interference by the police.

By 1920, Fritz was sent to Russia by the German oil industry to protect their investments and to investigate a new German military interest that had been acquired through a secret treaty. Germany would provide military training for the Red Army in exchange for training areas in Russia to conduct military maneuvers, which was prohibited by the Treaty of Versailles. Fritz soon began to clandestinely funnel funds to the Reds while he supported the White Armies. When the White Armies collapsed, he became a German military contact.

It was during his time in the Soviet Union that he met American industrialist Henry Ford, and he realized that the West was where the real financial action was going to take place. Fritz shifted his interests to the western parts of Europe and Germany, where there was money to be made from the Dawes and Young Plans for clever businessmen. Once back in Germany, Fritz joined the Nazi Party, and his talent for raising funds was quickly noticed by the German banking institutions.

Meanwhile, in Italy, Mussolini had shown that strong, daring leadership could easily control national government. His march on Rome was more successful because of a weak government rather than daring leadership. Mussolini had stayed close to the boarder in case things went south. When the government capitulated, Mussolini rushed to Rome to walk in front of the parade.

The Nazis attempted the Beer Hall putsch, and Hitler lost the first round of the struggle.

After the attempt, General Ludendorff, the hero of the Great War who marched with Hitler, surrendered right away and was allowed to walk away from the attempt to overthrow the government. Hitler was arrested and allowed to give long speeches during the trial that were broadcast over the radio. This took a local issue and made it national, increasing Hitler's popularity. He was sentenced to prison with his secretary and cook, where he wrote his book *Mein Kampf* (*My Struggle*).

Fritz moved up in the party and moved completely into the legitimate banking world as a major player. By 1926, he was a member of a semisecret organization of German businessmen called the Thule Society, and he was sent to the United States to study Detroit and Wall Street.

In the US, Fritz was able to study Henry Ford's business skills. Ford's factories were run by heartless task masters with stopwatches who enforced discipline by using spies and informants. Ford's control of the production process, from rubber plants in South America to lumber stands in North America, allowed the Model T to roll off the assembly line at the fastest rate in the world. Fritz marveled at how the American business world moved quickly to fill the production gap caused by the war and to increase the technology of the factories. IT&T, GE, Standard Oil, IBM, banking institutions, chemical and steel industries, even the Hoover vacuum cleaner had become so ingrained in British society that a vacuum was called a Hoover.

When the Nazi Party came to power in 1933, Fritz went back to Germany and took over a small bank from its former Jewish owners, who had become enemies of the state. The Nuremburg laws denied rights to Jewish citizens, and slowly began to prohibit all contact between Germans and Jews. A Jewish business owner could be charged with nearly any imaginable crime and his property would be confiscated and sold for a small price.

During the Olympic Games of 1936, two American Jewish runners were not allowed to run and missed their chance to win gold medals. The head of the American committee said that they did not want to embarrass the German government after Hitler refused to meet African American winners. The government had removed all negative signs of anti-Semitism during the games. After the games, the anti-Semitism returned, and the Fritz small bank became a major player in the financial world of Germany.

When World War II started, Fritz moved money from the conquered territories into German business interest and friends of German business. He sterilized the money with an extended route through France, Switzerland, Spain, Argentina, Mexico, Panama, and finally the United States.

Chapter 26

Volksabstimmung in Österreich—issued April 8, 1938

July 4, 1937, at 8:30 a.m.—Upstate New York

Mr. Charles M. Moody sat in his backyard planning how he was going to save his bank from that Bolshevik FDR. He would have to play both sides against each other and go into FDR's New Deal socialism until the times changed and a new power took over the government. The plan included his son, Rudy.

"Rudy, my boy, it is time for you to enter the world of business. You and I are off for a small trip today."

"Dad, I am still in college! I do not have time for business."

"I am afraid you do…or no more college. We are in a struggle for our future, and I need you now."

"What are you talking about, Dad?"

"We have to keep the others off balance and divided, and to do that, we need influence. This weekend, you and I are going to a political rally in the countryside, and I want you to stay in the background and watch and listen. Do not talk to anyone, and stay away from cameras."

"Why the big secret?"

"It is not a secret, son. I do not want to have you associated with any negative or adverse positions that could be an embarrassment later, that's all."

"But if these people are right, why not support them in the open?"

"Choosing sides is always dangerous. And in banking, it is wise money that always follows the power."

Later that afternoon, Moody and his son joined fellow countrymen at the parade. The platform and the parade field were surrounded by American flags, giving the impression of a sea of red, white, and blue on a canvas of green mountains. Men uniformed in black pants, white shirts, black leather belts, and diagonal straps over a shoulder were lined up in ranks on one side of the field and women on the other. In the back, a youth battalion and drum corps marked time as the speakers entered the rally to preach about the problematic direction America was heading and how new strong leadership could save the country from economic and moral decay.

At the end of the speeches, Charles walked over to shake the hand of Werner Hoffmann, a German banker. "Nice to see you again, Mr. Hoffmann. I hear your son is making a name for himself in the financial world in Germany. I hope all is well with him."

"Yes, he is. And on my return to Germany next month, I will give him your regards."

"Thank you! He has a good head on his shoulders and a good family heritage. Now do you think this group has much of a chance in this country?"

"No! But it is best to keep a lot of irons in the fire," replied Hoffmann.

"I could not agree more."

"Good, because I represent a group of German and Italian industrialists and bankers that wants to plan for various possibilities in the future and, shall we say, has funds that need to be invested. We are thinking your bank may be our bank."

"My business interest is business, Mr. Hoffmann, and nothing more. Any political interests that interfere with business are bad for business. Look at the Soviet Union with all its natural resources. That country has failed to provide its population with a modern consumer society. No, we need to control the institutions that try to stop business from developing."

"Yes, that is why my group of business associates wants to develop an unofficial network of business contacts, and they are willing to begin with a high level of investment. Is that an offer that you might consider, Mr. Moody?"

"Mr. Hoffmann, I am a businessman. What do you say we get our feet wet? I am sure we can become very good unofficial partners."

"I am glad to hear you say that. This envelope contains some Swiss, Spanish, and British bank accounts that you can transfer to your bank. I think 1938 will be a good year for your bank."

"Mr. Hoffmann, I think we will definitely have a good future together."

Chapter 27

Harding Overprint—issued May 1, 1929

In 1929, the postmaster said that $200,000 in stamps had been stolen.

The suggestion was made to overprint stamps for each state. This was rejected except in Nebraska and Kansas. The overprints caused confusion, as some postmasters thought that the overprinted stamps could only be used in the states indicated on the stamps. Overprints were used for many reasons; the most common were surcharges, commemorative and security measures.

Eastern Kansas, 1939

Gladys Hoff stepped onto the Greyhound bus heading for San Diego, California. Oscar "Dusty" Hoff, Gladys's sixteen-year-old brother, looking into the bus, saw her take a seat and waved to her through the window. She opened the window to say one last farewell:

"Dusty, I will write as soon as I get settled. I love you!"

"I love you too, sis," Dusty called as the bus pulled away from the station.

Just before Gladys boarded the bus, he had handed her an envelope. "Here, take this money. I do not need anything and you may. It is not much, but it is all I have. Take care, sis. I love you."

Gladys smiled, kissed him on the cheek, and gave him a big hug. "You are the best brother. As soon as I can, I'll send for you...I promise."

As the bus pulled away, Dusty could not help but feel a great loss. Gladys was his only link to the life they had once known.

The Hoff farm had once been a happy place for Gladys and Dusty. But in 1935, a horse kicked John Hoff in the head, and he died three days later. Their mother had died in childbirth with Dusty, so John had made a will that gave his brother Bryan the farm with the understanding that he would provide for the children and take care of the farm until Dusty turned twenty-one.

Bryan Hoff was the Ford dealer in town, and the Depression had cut deeply into his business and style of life. So with the death of his older brother, he moved his family out of their hometown and into his brother's larger farmhouse just outside of town. Bryan's wife, Gloria saw the move as a step down in the social ladder, but Bryan saw himself as a gentlemen farmer with a built-in work force in John's offspring.

Gladys and Dusty understood that the rules had changed on the very first day. Gloria always served her two kids, Eugene and Doris, the largest share of anything that was divided, and Dusty always was given the smallest piece. Gladys was one of the prettiest girls in the county, so there was always a steady stream of boys at the door with small gifts, which never sat well with Doris or Gloria. To even the score, Gladys was never given new clothes or new shoes. Instead, she wore Doris's hand-me-downs and became known as the second-best dresser in school, which was not intended as a compliment.

Dusty, who was younger and bigger than Bryan's son, Eugene, did not have to worry about hand-me-downs, but he was never allowed to have more than two shirts and overalls at a time. When Dusty won the spelling bee and Eugene came in second, Gloria saw to it that Dusty had chores to do late into the night every time there was a competition so that he would be too tired to win another spelling bee. Any time Dusty outplayed Eugene, his workload increased. Gloria's disdain combined with Bryan's constant scheming made life intolerable for both Dusty and Gladys.

Gladys and Dusty had planned to save their money and leave together, but Gladys convinced Dusty that there was a faster way out of the situation if she could go to California and get a good job and then send for him. She left for California the day after her eighteenth birthday. She made her own cake, and as she started to cut it, Dusty sang out in a loud voice, "Happy birthday to you! Happy birthday to you! Happy birthday, dear Gladys!" The others joined in but without much enthusiasm.

"Blow out the candles, Gladys. I want a piece of cake," Dusty said.

"Here is your present, Gladys," Doris said with a big cat grin as she handed Gladys a wrapped package.

Gladys laid down the cake knife and opened the present. "What is this? This is your old Sunday dress, Doris! If this doesn't take the cake…not only did I have to make my own birthday cake, but I get another hand-me-down dress from Doris! What a birthday!"

"There are a lot of people in this community who would be glad to get that dress! You should be thankful and happy with what you have, young lady," Gloria said angrily.

"What do I have? A farm that my father built into the best farm in the county and has been allowed to run down over the last six years while you and your family buy and do whatever you want! Plus, I have been given old hand-me-down clothes from the 'princess' here and always treated as though I'm a burden. Well, I'm eighteen today, and I have an interview for a job at the bank tomorrow, and soon I will have my own money."

"That's very nice, my dear, but you must remember what we have given up to take care of you and your brother these past few years. We did it because blood is thicker than water. Your father trusted us to do the right thing. Money is tight right now, or have you not noticed that there is a depression in this country?" Gloria said smugly.

"That's real funny, Gloria! Doris has plenty of new dresses. All I wanted was a new dress for my job interview!" Gladys said.

"Well, I would buy you a new dress if the money was there… but it is not, and that is that. So forget it!" Bryan said firmly.

"I will not forget it! You have been living on our farm for six years and living a pretty good life as far as I can see, Uncle!"

"You watch your mouth, young lady!" said Gloria.

"You watch YOUR mouth you, stuck-up bitch. You have been cheating us since the very first day you moved into this house."

"That is enough, Gladys! Or else!" yelled Bryan.

"Or else WHAT, you overinflated gasbag! I am eighteen, and I'm leaving this place the first thing in the morning. I am tired of picking up and cleaning for the both of you and your selfish brats."

"I cannot believe that you would treat us this way after all we have given up to take care of you and Dusty. You are nothing but an ungrateful little tramp, with all those young men running after you in heat! I can't believe it! We ought to—" said Gloria.

"You ought to what, you old dried-up cow?"

"Gladys, you are a mean, selfish girl. This conversation is finished!" Bryan said as he took Gloria's arm and walked out of the room.

"What are you going to do?" Dusty asked his sister.

"I'm going upstairs to pack. Then first thing in the morning, I'm going into town to catch a bus for California."

"I'll go with you," Dusty said excitedly.

"No, we can't make it together. I'll go and send for you once I have a job. There's a lot of defense industry work starting up out there because of the war scare in Europe. I have a high school diploma, and

I can type faster than any of the other girls in town. I promise—I will send for you when I have enough money and a place for us to stay."

"I wish I could go with you," Dusty said.

"I know, but you are only sixteen. Gloria and Bryan would pitch a fit if they lost their free labor for the farm. And we only have enough money saved for one bus ticket…"

So the next morning, Dusty took Gladys to the Greyhound bus stop just in time to buy a ticket. As Dusty watched the bus roll down the street, he felt completely alone for the first time in his life. He was thinking about "blood is thicker than water," and it sure was only some blood seemed to be thicker in families. Money seemed to make blood thicker. People in town knew what Bryan was doing to his brother's children with little acts of kindness, but did not dare to get on the wrong side of Bryan and his money friends.

Chapter 28

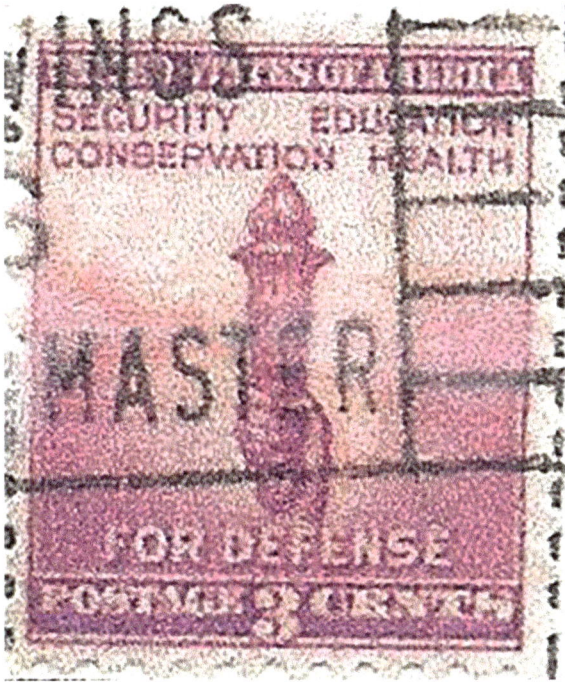

**Security, Education, Conservation, Health
for Defense——issued October 16, 1940**

This stamp was Franklin Delano Roosevelt's effort to move the American mindset from isolation to defense. October 16, 1940, was the deadline to sign up for the draft, and the National Defense Stamps Series was intended to keep the need for defense at the forefront.

October 1941—San Diego, California

Gladys found a job working in a bank and wrote Dusty once a month about how close she was to sending for him. Yet any money left at the end of the month she spent on clothes.

Whenever she felt a pang of guilt, she reminded herself that a woman who had plans to be in management needed the right clothes. Dusty was young. He would understand her needs. She was learning that men were nothing but bigger boys. All they needed was a bit more encouragement and reassurance for them to do what she wanted.

One day as she walked up to her apartment, she saw a sailor sitting on the porch. It took a few seconds before she realized that the tall man standing in front of her was her brother, Dusty.

"Dusty? Dusty!" she yelled as she threw her arms around him.

"Hey, I can't breathe!"

"Oh, shut up! I can't believe this! What has happened to you?"

"Well, after you left, Bryan started to knock me around anytime he got into a mood. One day I had enough, so I hit back."

"What happened?"

"Let me tell you the whole story. It's a good one! One day, Bryan, Eugene, and I were all in the south field trying to pull a stump out. We had a chain wrapped around it, and Bryan told Eugene to take up the slack. Eugene stepped on the gas and let out the clutch, forgetting that the tractor was in reverse. He was coming right at us! Bryan jumped to the side and went face first into a cow pie. Somehow Eugene got the tractor right over the stump and went full speed into the creek. There were the two of them—Eugene with his face white as a ghost and his boots full of muddy creek water and Bryan with his face covered in cow pie. As we walked back to the house, Bryan did not say one word while Eugene made excuses about how it was not his fault. I was laughing the whole way back."

"You're making this up," Gladys said between giggles.

"Wait—it gets better! When we got back to the barn, Bryan turned to me and said, 'This is all your fault.' He took a swing at me and hit Eugene in the side of the head, which made me laugh even harder. The next thing I knew, they were both throwing punches at me. I ducked under Eugene's swing and hit him with an upper cut that turned his lights out. Bryan was a little harder to handle. He hit me when I was busy with Eugene. The punch landed on my jaw. I thought it was broken at first. I could see a smile on his face through all the cow manure and started to laugh again. That seemed to make him furious, and he came running right at me. I let go with a hay-maker that hit him right on the chin. Down he went—like a sack of spuds."

"Then what did you do?"

"I checked to see if they were okay, and then I walked into the house to pack my stuff. I was almost done when Aunt Gloria came storming into my room yelling that she would have me arrested. I walked out of the house with her still yelling at me. I hitchhiked to Kansas City and two days later walked into the Navy recruiter's office, where I lied about my age and joined up. I'll be eighteen this month anyway. So here I am."

"I'm so sorry, Dusty, I should have worked harder," Gladys said, hugging her brother again.

"Nah, it's not your fault. Things happen, and you learn to live with it."

"Why didn't you write and tell me how bad things were?"

"What could you have done, come back? That would not have done any good. And besides, I like the Navy. They're sending me to the new homeport in Hawaii. The government moved the Pacific Fleet there from the West Coast to show the Japanese that we mean business. I'm assigned to the USS *West Virginia*. That's a battleship, and they call a battle wagon. It's not the newest ship in the Navy, but it's bigger than those tin-can destroyers. There are some five thousand men on board, and if there is any trouble, we can give them the business. By the way, I have named you to get my allotment pay so I can save some money. Is that alright with you?"

"Of course," Gladys said, looking at Dusty incredulously. "I just can't believe it's you!"

"Well, if you're so happy to see me, how about taking me out for something to eat? I'm starving!"

"Give me just one minute. I just have to make a phone call and cancel a date."

"I'm sorry, I did not think about you having plans for this evening. We can do it tomorrow night."

"Are you sure? It will only take a minute. After all, you are my brother, and I haven't seen you in forever!"

"No, keep your date. I will come by about seven tomorrow night to pick you up, and we will have a nice dinner on me. I have my own money now, and the government gives me a bed and as much food as I can eat. Talk about the good life."

The next day Dusty picked up Gladys, and they went to the waterfront for dinner. She was wearing a new dress and high heels and was very striking and turned heads when they walked into the restaurant.

"I think I am the most envied man in here tonight," said Dusty.

"What makes you say that?"

"Every man in the place is looking at you—that's why!"

"Oh, Dusty you are such a joker."

"Now, you know your effect on the male species, Gladys. So do not tell anyone I am your brother."

"Why?"

"There are a couple of guys from my recruit class and also headed for Pearl and the West Virginia. I'll be the talk of the ship when the word of the gorgeous woman I had dinner with the night before I left for Pearl."

The rest of the night Gladys played her part to make Dusty's legend grow.

Chapter 29

Win the War—issued July 4, 1942

Franklin Delano Roosevelt did not want the war-related stamps to be militaristic. One newspaper said the stamp was not a symbol of victory but one of pacifism, since the eagle and arrows are facing different directions.

December 7, 1941, at 7:51 a.m.— on board the West Virginia, BB48

Sunday mornings at Pearl Harbor were lazy times. The whole place relaxed after the Saturday night football game and a night in town. Dusty had reported for duty on November 1 and was assigned a duty station topside on the bridge. This separated him from the snipes, the crew members who worked below deck.

Dusty was proud to be on the *West Virginia*, BB48. It was a small city, with barbershops, a clothing store, tailor shops, a library, a bakery, a galley, a movie theater, and a gee dunk, where he could buy ice cream and milkshakes. The ship even had its own newspaper. With all its amenities for the crew, the *West Virginia* was also a floating fortress. The ship had just been fitted with blisters, a thin skin that was designed to prevent torpedo damage to the ship's double bottom hull, which was divided into numerous watertight compartments. The ship was 624 feet long and 97 feet, 6 inches wide, with 28,900 horsepower that allowed her to hit a speed of twenty-one knots with four screws. She had eight sixteen-inch .45-caliber guns in four turrets. Each shell for the gun weighed 2,300 pounds and could throw a shell twenty-two miles. The armaments also included multiple .51-caliber secondary battery guns and .25-caliber antiaircraft battery guns. The massive ship was impressive by all standards.

The West Virginia was tied next to the Tennessee in Battleship Row. Forward of the West Virginia were the Maryland and Oklahoma, and aft was the Arizona. The fleet had been moved earlier to Pearl Harbor to send a message to Japan that the US was the power in the Pacific. So as Dusty lay in his bunk in the crew quarters of the battleship, he was feeling comfortable and confident.

"Sam, how's your head today?" Dusty asked as another sailor groaned from a nearby bunk.

"I think I'm okay," Sam responded. "But I just don't remember how I got back to the ship!"

"I carried you," Dusty said. "And you need to lose some weight if I'm going to have to do that again."

"I'm sorry I got drunk like that. I guess that Dear John letter really got to me. What made me so mad was that the guy my girl is now in love with was my best friend!"

"I know the story, Sam. You repeated it over and over...all the way back to the ship."

Their conversation was interrupted by a series of muffled explosions.

An alarm sounded throughout the ship. "General quarters! This is not a drill!"

Dusty and Sam raced to the hatchway and their battle stations. Dusty started up the ladder toward the deck and was hit by the feet of a sailor who came sliding down, thinking it was the down ladder. Dusty picked himself up from the metal floor and headed up the ladder again. This time he made it topside and headed for his battle station on the bridge. A loud explosion made him cover his ears as a bomb hit the *Tennessee*, BB43. Fragments from the explosion tore into the bridge of the *West Virginia*. Dusty watched in horror as he saw the captain fall, covered with blood.

Dusty looked out into the harbor and saw nothing but Jap planes. *They are destroying us!* Dusty thought. Everything seemed to be slow motion as he stood and gaped at the sight. There were groans of agony all around him. Arms and legs seemed to be doing an ugly dance searching desperately for their bodies. Dusty was frozen for a moment, unable to think what he should do as waves of terror and nausea washed over him.

"You, sailor...sailor!" an officer yelled. "Start helping the wounded. And get a move on it! We are at WAR!"

"Aye-aye, sir!" Dusty responded, moving toward the injured man closest to him.

"I need you to come with me now," another officer barked, leading Dusty and another sailor to a launch. "There are men out there in the water, and we've got to pick them up before the fire gets to them." The diesel fuel leaking from the broken battleships was congealing in the cold water of the Pacific and the men who had fallen into the water. Dusty could hear the screams as the fiery ships ignited the fuel and the sailors who were engulfed in it.

They were picking men out of the water when the *Arizona* went up in a cloud of smoke. The shock wave from the blast was deafening and almost caused Dusty to fall overboard. *There are 1,200 men in there!* he thought in horror as he pulled a Marine called a bell-hop into the boat. Dusty was still pulling men from the water as the *Utah* capsized. A second wave of Japanese planes targeted the *Nevada* not long after. The crew beached the ship to protect the harbor.

"Where the HELL are our planes?" an ensign yelled to no one and turned the boat to pick up another sailor. A Japanese plane buzzed overhead so close that Dusty could see the pilot laughing at the damage and destruction he was causing.

Many hours later, when all who could be saved had been, Dusty was relieved of duty for the day. Exhausted, he could barely move, but his mind raced as he thought about the events of the day. *The impossible had happened. The American fleet had been completely crippled. How would they ever rebuild?*

But Dusty and his fellow sailors were resilient, and so was the US Navy. Dusty was soon assigned to the USS *Enterprise*, where he worked with a ring knocker, one of the many new Annapolis graduates that filled the officer ranks to replace those who had fallen at Pearl Harbor. By the time of the Battle of Midway, Dusty had made chief and won the Silver Star and two Bronze Stars. He was recommended for the Navy Cross for action at the Battle of Midway.

Though Dusty was honored by the recognition, he realized that promotions and medals were being handed out like candy. America needed to keep its Navy staffed and motivated if they were going to win the war.

The Navy's perseverance was shown most vividly when on May 17, 1942, the *West Virginia* was refloated. Inspections showed that she had suffered seven torpedo hits. More than sixty bodies were discovered, including those of three men who had been trapped in an air pocket. They survived on battle rations and water, keeping log until December 23, 1941. They were the last victims of the attack on Pearl Harbor.

Chapter 30

Chinese Resistance—issued July 7, 1942

This stamp was intended to bolster the people of China against the Japanese that invaded China on July 7, 1937. The stamp is emblazoned with the images of Abraham Lincoln and Sun Yat-sen with the words "Fight the war and build the country" written in Chinese characters. The stamp was issued at Denver, Colorado, the place where Sun Yat-sen left the United States to become the president of the Republic of China.

Long Beach, California, 1946

Gladys was marrying for a second time, this time to a banker named Rudy Moody. The first marriage ended with the death of her husband, a Navy chief who had also sent her his allotment check, which had allowed her to live the life she wanted and find a rich husband.

Dusty came home to find that his uncle had lost the farm by taking out large loans that he couldn't repay. Rather than risk his own business, he had arranged a planned foreclosure and cut his brother's children out of their rightful inheritance. The loans had been taken out in January of 1942 to buy farms for his son and son-in-law to give them deferments from military service.

Bryan went to work on the railroad and sat on the Selective Service board for the county, sending many of the town's boys off to war.

Gladys had been a war widow for a little more than a year, and the death benefit money had just about run out. To maintain her lifestyle, she started using Dusty's money. Dusty would want her to use it. Besides what was he going to do with it? She had to keep up appearances if she was going to get remarried. But not to another sailor. That was for sure.

One day Gladys and her friend Kitty decided to go to the beach. Kitty was wearing red short shorts and a white blouse that was tied in a knot in the front. Gladys had on a yellow blouse tied the same way and a pair of tan shorts. For Kitty and Gladys, going to the beach was sitting in an upscale bar on Pacific Coast Highway with view of the ocean. Gladys always had a martini because that was the drink of the "in" crowd. Kitty was a beer and whisky girl.

As they sipped their drinks at the bar, both women saw the handsome man in a booth. He noticed them as well and headed toward them. "My, he is handsome" Kitty said.

"He sure is!" Gladys replied.

Kitty almost jumped off her stool and started to walk toward him, meeting halfway with her best "I'm available" walk.

"Hi," he said and walked past her.

Kitty stood with her hands on her hips looking at him in shock.

Gladys could not help but laugh at the sight of it and was startled when he stopped in front of her. "I know you will not believe this," he said, looking Gladys straight in the eye, "but I'm in town for a dinner meeting tonight, and I do not want to go without you."

"But I don't even know you."

"I can fix that. Hello, I am Rudy, and you are?"

And that is how Gladys found her second husband, Rudy. And it was worth spending a bit of money to find a great man like Rudy, even if some of the money belonged to Dusty. After all, Dusty had been saving for farm equipment, and Bryan had foreclosed on the farm when Dusty was still in the Navy.

Dusty had written her often from the war. The nightmare of Pearl Harbor had been followed by battles in the Coral Sea and Midway. The worst had been at Guadalcanal, where his ship was sunk at night in one of the worst defeats in American naval history. As he was abandoning ship, a seaman from below decks had grabbed part of the ship's structure with both arms wrapped around it and held on tight and would not let go. The seaman stood there, frozen to the ship like a white ghost with eyes as big as pie tins. Dusty tried to pull him off the ship, but his arms were locked too tight. In a desperate move, Dusty hit the man in the head trying to break his arms free, but the grip became tighter.

Dusty kept trying until he was ordered by an officer to abandon the frightened sailor. He and the rest of the men had jumped into the sea, swimming away from the sinking ship. But Dusty had written to his sister he just couldn't forget the man's terrified face.

Chapter 31

Thirteenth Amendment—issued October 20, 1940

This stamp was commissioned to commemorate the passage of the Thirteenth Amendment. Franklin Delano Roosevelt suggested that the stamp be issued at the New York World's Fair. The statue pictured on the stamp is called Emancipation. Proofs of the stamp were presented to Joe Louis, Marian Anderson, and Bojangles by Postmaster General Frank Walker.

August 10, 2001—on the road to Big Bear, California

Congressman Robert T. Chase did not like the mountains because he did not like to be out of touch with people. He needed them more than they needed him, but most of them did not realize it. His fear of people not liking him kept him in a constant state of motion, working the crowd and trying to win the favor of those around him. One week it would be blue suits that made him more appealing, and the next week any suit with a red tie after someone told him that red was a power color.

The congressman had discovered that handshakes could send different meanings. A strong grip was a sign of leadership, while a handshake with the second hand touching an elbow projected a feeling of warmth and caring. The congressman was a political animal, and the modern world had made him a more efficient predator as he continually sought votes and approval.

Congressman Chase had been elected right after World War II. His family had money, and he increased his wealth during the war. That, along with his good looks and his keen sense of what motivated people, made him a good local politician. The only thing he lacked was a war record, and the best political jobs after the war went to men who had served. Time, however, was on his side. The anticommunism campaign was a sure ticket to higher office. The congressman was no rabid red-baiter as many were at the time. He believed that the communists were evil and must be defeated, but not at the cost of American rights.

This was just one sign of his political aptitude. He always made people look at both sides of the issue and then pushed them to make a decision based on good old-fashioned common sense rather than emotions or passion. His use of language allowed him to easily manipulate people's emotions, and an adept salesman, Chase could sell his opinion to nearly anyone.

Congressman Chase had started in the family business in 1945, selling televisions to people who did not have electric service. The family had made a fortune after WWI, allowing Robert to get elected to Congress in 1949 and went right to work protecting his family's interests.

Chase's greatest common-sense victory was his protection of German industry. It was Hitler's regime, not the industrialist, who used slave labor. Yes, it was true that some industrialists did support the Nazis, but that was only at the beginning when they were fooled, as were many American industrialists, such as Henry Ford and Charles Lindberg. We would not call them Nazis. He pointed out that we needed the German industrialists to fight communism or we might lose the American Dream. That line of thinking won them over every time.

The congressman and other politicians, industrialists, and businessmen had found it easy to shift blame to radicals and fringe elements to remove their own culpability. Each time the Nazis past came up, the threat they presented was pushed deeper and deeper into the shadows. The only thing that remained as a permanent reminder was the Holocaust, as people quickly forgot about the corrupt political and economic systems. After all, it was only the Nazis around Hitler that were the villains, not the German laws, political leaders, business leaders, military leaders, soldiers, or even the military rank and file. They had also been victims of corrupt leadership. The proof could be seen in the fact that men from Germany's paramilitary groups were able to hold political offices as in international leadership and in the United Nations without very much public outcry.

Today, the Cold War was over and the Russian Empire was broken apart, and the new republics were converting to capitalism. Nixon and Reagan had been right. This century was the American century.

The congressman's thoughts came to an end as he drove up to William Steiner's cabin.

Bill came out onto the porch and waited for him to get out of the car. They had known each other since 1945.

"Hi, Bob. What's the emergency?"

"Heidi is dead," Robert replied. "She's been dead for two or three days of natural causes. I sent Eric and Carl over to pick up that damn album of hers, and it was gone."

"Gone?"

"Yes, gone. That greedy little landlord found it and sold it for the rent. Gene and Carl went by his house and asked a few questions. He told them he sold it to a coin dealer in town. Before they left the landlord's house, Carl broke the landlord's neck and threw him down the basement stairs so it looked like a fall. Everything looks good and clean from that end."

"Then we have the album back?"

"No. They went to the coin shop, and it was closed. So they asked a few questions and went by the shop owner's house to wait. He showed up just after dark. They approached him, and he started to get overly excited. Carl overreacted and killed him. They did pick up the keys to the shop and emptied the cash register of cash, checks, and charge card receipts."

"Did they get the album?"

"No."

"We'd better find that album, or we've lost the whole network," Steiner said. "Did those two bozos find any leads?"

"They picked up an album, but it was the wrong one. So we'll go through the cash register receipts and see what we can uncover."

"Look on the bright side. Nobody is going to look for a code, let alone break the code. Our biggest concern right now is that whoever has the album will sell it off in parts. If that happens, we will lose the records of the network."

"That code is Schutzstaffel numbers, and they can be traced. That's the point. Though the SS is not a threat to most people, we need to protect the identity of its members."

"Who cares anymore," Steiner said with a shrug. "Maybe a few old Jews and some radical liberals. And even if they do figure out it's filled with SS records, what could anyone even do with that information? Let's just look carefully at the organization to see if there are any old links to the past that can get away from us and cause problems. When this is over, you need to get started on that, understand? And don't send those fools again. Find someone reliable to use."

Chapter 32

**Brandenburger tor mit Reichsadler—
issued January 26, 1943**

August 11, 2001—a café on a desolate highway

Congressman Chase walked into the café and over to the booth where Steiner sat. The café was right out of the 1950s, with red vinyl-covered stools and booth seats. The floor was black and white linoleum, and there were ads on the walls that had not been changed in years.

The congressman ordered coffee and toast. As soon as the waitress walked away, Bill asked, "How is the hunt going?"

"Those buffoons can't find it. They've been through the list twice."

"How many are on the list?"

"Three. They were the only people who used charge cards that day. The only one who could have bought the album has already been checked out. Plus, they went to his home and got his album. It wasn't the one we're looking for."

William looked out the window as he asked, "Did our people ever question this guy?"

"No. He is an investigator of some type and is never in one place for long. And we didn't want to attract his attention."

"What made you believe he has the album?"

"He wrote a check to the coin shop owner for five thousand dollars."

"When did they search his house?"

"Early the next day. He was not home."

"It is not hard to believe that a stamp collector would already have an album like the one we are looking for. He may have even put it in a bank or safety deposit box. We better find this guy fast!"

"Why?"

"I have three good reasons," Steiner said firmly. "One, he's a stamp collector. Two, he is an investigator. And three, that book could place our organization and the people we represent in jeopardy. If they are in jeopardy, then we become the problem at the same time. We do not want to take the chance that he will put anything together."

"I thought the album was not a major problem..." the congressman said, trailing off as he realized Steiner might not be pleased with the accusation.

"That was when it was in the hands of an ordinary Joe, not someone whose job is investigation and find answers to complex questions."

"Then I'll get right on it."

Steiner looked at the congressman, seeing that the politician was already thinking of ways to control his part of the situation if things went south. The fool believed he held the power if there came a time to correct the situation; the congressman would be the first to know how the problem was solved. For now, the congressman was still a useful tool for the organization.

Chapter 33

Transcontinental Railroad—issued May 10, 1944

This stamp was commissioned to commemorate the seventy-fifth anniversary of the completion of the transcontinental railroad at Promontory Point, Utah, and the driving of the golden spike on May 10, 1869. As soon as it was issued, questions about the smoke and flag going in different directions were raised.

On a train in New Mexico, 1945

Thomas Bowpin walked down the aisle in his crisp, pressed conductor's uniform, his eyes scanning the passengers as he called out, "Tickets, please." Thomas wore his uniform as if he were in the military, and he was proud of his contribution to the war effort. In 1939, he had been a milkman when the war broke out in Europe, and he knew the US would be pulled into the war. After a systematic study of his options, Thomas went to work for the railroad industry in November of 1939 because, as Thomas saw it, the railroads were important to the national defense and so were the men who worked on it. Those workers would be exempt from the draft.

By 1943, Thomas had polished his way up to conductor. His personal mission was to catch draft dodgers and deserters. He had become somewhat of a hero on his run for notifying the military authorities of five deserters in the last three months. He would often retell the stories at family gatherings, where his wife's father sat at the table beaming with pride at his patriotic son-in-law. This same man had protected his own sons from military service by dividing the large family farm into smaller farms that were large enough to make each son exempt from military service. The sons were doing their part by flying large American flags on their farms "to support the boys over there" and by living vicariously through Thomas's railway efforts.

Thomas knew that his stories were a bit fanciful. The first four soldiers were drunk and missed their stop. Thomas was asleep and failed to call out the stop, so the soldiers did not get off the train until a few stops further down the line, where a now awakened Thomas pointed them out as deserters, partly to cover the fact that he had been asleep himself.

The fifth deserter was a young boy of nineteen, whose only relative was his sick and dying mother. He had jumped ship when the Navy was too slow in giving him emergency leave. As the young boy got closer to home, his nerves and worry over his mother caused him to confide in Thomas. When Thomas retold the story, he always omitted the details of the sick mother and the young man's age.

"Tickets, please," Thomas called as he made his way down the train, scanning for young men who might make good additions to his repertoire of stories. Three passengers on this trip had caught Thomas's attention. While he could not place his finger on the reason, something about this little group was not right. As the train passed through the New Mexico countryside, he heard one of the men swear in German, which was not unusual in itself. After all, Thomas's own grandfather was from Germany and sometimes used German words to express anger. What made this unusual was that another one of the men responded with a sharp "nein," the kind of dissent only a German would use. *I'd better keep an eye on these three,* Thomas thought, his excitement growing.

Eric Wolfgang Rossmann noticed the unusual attention the conductor was paying to their trio. Eric had joined the Hitler Youth in 1932 and had been loyal to the party ever since. By 1939, he was working in the euthanasia program to rid Germany of inferior individuals with mental retardation and birth defects. The notices given to the grieving relatives listed the deaths as pneumonia or other common diseases. But Eric was administering lethal injections into the victims to rid the country of defective human beings. However, soon public outcry halted the program, so Eric had entered the Death Squads, the Einsatzgruppen. He now worked to rid the world of the vermin Judenräte and Bolshevism.

Eric was assigned to group C when Operation Barbarossa was launched on June 22, 1941. The Death Squads did not go in with the frontline troops. Eric and his group came behind, looking for the enemy in order to eliminate them. To Eric, extermination was not murder, since it was not done in anger. The state had the right to take a life that was a threat to itself or its sanctity. Eric saw himself as the agent of the state, only eliminating danger.

Eric had been calm and purposeful when he and the Einsatzgruppen entered the first small village just across the border in Russian-held Poland. Jews and any other individuals suspected of partisan activities were walked out of the village to a ditch and shot in the back of the head. By the time the group reached Babi Yar in Kiev, they had refined their skill. They could kill as many as thirty-three thousand individuals in a very short time span. Eric felt the same calm, cool purposefulness as he sat on the train awaiting his next mission.

"Ticket, please," the conductor called, looking carefully at Eric. As the conductor exited the car to move to the next car, Eric quietly got up from his seat to follow. As was typical, the conductor took out his flashlight and shined it down onto the rail to look for sparks and gouges on the rail. This would help him to see if one of the wheels on the train was coming loose. As the conductor lowered his head to inspect the rails, a hand pushed firmly on his back. The conductor didn't have time to scream before the train crushed him beneath its wheels.

The conductor was missing, and a search was conducted on the train at the next station. A work crew found his body lying in the tracks. It was believed that he fell off the train while checking the wheels. The papers reported that a brave American hero had died doing his patriotic duty on the home front. That he was responsible for the discovery of a number of deserters. His hometown named a street after him on the next July Fourth celebration.

Chapter 34

Motion Pictures—issued October 31, 1944

This stamp was commissioned to commemorate the motion picture industry's efforts to boost morale at home and on the frontlines.

The design shows troops in an outdoor South Pacific setting.

August 15, 2001—Oroville, California

The nurse looked at the chart and then at the patient sitting in the chair. He was eighty years old and diagnosed with Alzheimer's disease. He had been in the home for six years and was only visited by his admitting physician, Dr. Claus Zimmermann, who came once a month. The Alzheimer's made the old man paranoid with auditory hallucinations. When the staff helped him shower, he would start screaming "Gas! Gas!" When a doctor approached him, he would yell, "Not me, you idiot—THEM." The nurse pitied the man, but she avoided him whenever she could. His behavior made her uneasy.

"How is our patient today?" Dr. Zimmermann asked the nurse.

"About the same as always. He is in the camps today as a guard. In the lunch line, he started yelling at the other patients to hurry up or they would all be liquidated and made into soap. And after lunch, he was a guard walking a small old lady to the killing pit. She slipped and fell, and he spoke to her softly, telling her it was all right. Then he went through the motions of shooting her in the back of the head and watching her fall into the pit."

"Yes, the delusions with the disease have taken him from being a survivor of the camps to being one of his tormentors. Everyday things we take for normal activity may trigger bad memories when the brain begins to lose its acuity," the doctor noted. "This role shift probably makes his life easier to understand and control."

"Well, that may be, but most of us really don't want to work with him any longer. He's pretty frightening! Sometimes he even attacks the staff."

"I will see about getting a private caregiver to sit with him during the day. Will that help relieve the staff's concerns?"

"That might help with some of the load. The people here love their patients, but not Mr. Rossmann. This is just a hard job to start with, and Mr. Rossmann and his hallucinations make the job that much more heart-wrenching."

"I understand," Dr. Zimmermann said. "I will see what I can do." Outside the home, Dr. Zimmermann made a phone call.

"It's Zimmermann here and we need to talk about Eric."

"What has happened?"

"He is getting worse, and I'll have someone come to sit in the room with him until we make a final decision."

"Okay, let me think about it for a day or two."

"It's your call," said Zimmermann.

Rossmann SS375082

Chapter 35

Swastika—issued January 18, 1934

1936 Olympic Stamps

The first issue was used as postage and the value today is in the unused stamps. The second issue of this series of stamps was saved and the value today is in the postmarked stamps.

August 16, 2001—Oroville, California

The front door of the rest home gave the impression of one of the best vacation spas in the country. The entry was polished to a high shine in the two waiting areas on each side of the information desk. The woman behind the desk was neatly dressed, with dyed reddish-orange hair that made her look older than she was. As CE approached the desk, she looked up with false concern and said, "May I help you?"

"Hello! My name is Mr. Hall. I have come to see a patient by the name of Eric Wolfgang Rossmann."

"Are you a relative?" the receptionist asked.

"No, I am an insurance investigator doing some research on a crime. Mr. Rossmann may be very helpful in filling in some details."

"He is in room 115 down the hall and to the left. You will have to check in with the nurse at the desk there. Just fill out the nametag and sign the log-book. Thank you."

C.E. quickly scribbled his name in the logbook and began walking down the hall. The corridor was filled with carts carrying patient meals and clean bed linens. A construction crew was working on the wiring in the wall at the far end of the corridor.

"Excuse me, I am looking for room 115."

"Number 115 is right there," a woman in pink pants said, pointing to the room across the hall. "The RN is in there with him right now."

As CE turned toward the room, a nurse came scurrying out followed by loud yelling in German. The only thing CE could make out was something about Jews.

"Hello, I am an insurance investigator and would like to ask Mr. Rossmann some questions, if he is up to it."

"Well, you can try," the nurse responded. "But Mr. Rossmann has Alzheimer's disease and lives in the past. He was in the death camps during World War II, and the trauma of that experience is reenacted in his mind continually. However, he remembers his role not as a camp survivor but as one of the guards that tormented him. He lost his whole family in the camps, and he must have seen some horrible things. So as you can imagine, he struggles to cope most of the time."

"Well, I'd still like to visit with him, if you don't mind," CE said politely to the nurse.

"I do not mind in the least. Dr. Zimmermann is his only visitor, and he only comes once a month. Poor Mr. Rossmann will probably enjoy the attention from someone other than the staff."

When they walked into Eric's room, a nurse was giving the eighty-year-old man a sponge bath. CE noticed the numbers tattooed on his arm, which were now misshapen on his sagging, aging skin. Rossmann noticed his gaze, smiled, and said "Hauptscharführer."

"What made you think this man was a Holocaust survivor?"

"Dr. Zimmermann is a close friend of his and told us the story."

"This man isn't a Holocaust survivor, I assure you," CE said to the nurse.

"How do you know?" she asked in a bewildered voice.

"Well, for one thing, he's never been circumcised."

"Then what about the tattoo?" the nurse asked, still bewildered.

"Jewish inmates were tattooed on the forearm where it was easy and fast to do," CE explained. "But Mr. Rossmann's tattoo is on his upper arm, precisely where SS members were marked. That tattoo number is SS375082, not 55375082. This man was a member of the Death Head SS."

"You mean that all those awful stories this old man was telling were real? He is a monster!" Both nurses looked at the old man with horror and revulsion as they walked out of the room. Eric Rossmann looked at CE carefully as the investigator walked toward him.

"I can tell you know things," Rossmann said to CE. "And I can tell you are looking for something. Well, I will tell you what you want to know. I have been here in Russia since the first Einsatzgruppen units started the T-4 program. This damn country is so big and cold that it takes forever for the Jews to dig the pits. We lost valuable time that first winter. I was always cold!"

"Do you think you are in Russia now?" CE asked.

"Of course! But Steiner is taking me out of this godforsaken place any day now so I can start on my next mission."

"And what is that?" CE asked with curiosity.

"My team and I will take a U-boat to the United States. We are being sent to kill someone in Georgia," Rossmann said with clarity. Then his eyes clouded. "Or maybe we already killed him. Yes, we did. We rode the train to get there. It was a wonderful ride except for the nosy conductor. I had to take care of him...somewhere in New Mexico, I think."

"Who were you sent to kill?" C.E. asked.

The man's eyes grew steely again. "I cannot tell you. Our mission is top secret! Only Heidi kept records."

"Who was Heidi? And what records, Eric?" CE said, his curiosity growing.

"Heidi knew everything. She was so good at numbers and facts in her little stamp book. If you wanted a name and wanted to know where he was from or where he was, Heidi knew. She didn't talk much, but she was a looker—and smarter than a whip."

"What was Heidi's full name, Eric?"

"Who are you? Why are you asking me all these questions? Get away from me or I'll have you sent to selection, you Jewish scum!"

CE walked out of the room and past the nurse's station. The bell for room 115 rang loudly, but the nurse pretended not to hear it. "Let the monster rot in hell!" he heard her mumble under her breath.

That night, a local radio station reported that old Mr. Rossmann was not a Holocaust survivor but a spy, and the morning paper ran with the headline "Nazi Hides in Rest Home as a Jew." And the next day when the nurse went in to check on Mr. Rossmann, it was discovered that he had died in his sleep. They tried to notify Dr. Zimmermann, but he could not be found.

Chapter 36

Hitler mit Kind—issued April 10, 1940

Spitler Stamp—a Cinderella stamp

This propaganda stamp pictured a child spitting in Hitler's face. The printing was done by a civilian stamp dealer in Los Angeles, California, for profit. Lawrence & Graves printed the stamps, and they were used in the mail. The secret service confiscated the stamp stock, plates, and production supplies. Later the stamps were reissued without names or date.

August 18, 2001—Seal Beach, California

CE was sitting in a local sports bar talking with Benjamin Franklin about his visit with Rossmann.

"I'll tell you, Ben, the whole staff believed that the old guy was a camp survivor who was reliving his life as a guard instead of as a Jewish prisoner to cope with his trauma. This Dr. Zimmermann had told the story that Rossmann was a Holocaust survivor, and they just accepted it. They missed the evidence right in front of them that he was not a Jew."

"Well, political correctness sometimes makes people afraid to ask sensitive questions. After all, they wouldn't want to offend him."

"Nevertheless, I was surprised. Just because a doctor tells you something, you believe it to be the indisputable truth, even if you see an inconsistency?"

"Why are you surprised, CE? We call it spin today, but in the 1930s, it was the Big Lie. Someone said all it takes is a big lie with a little bit of truth in it to change history. The funny thing is, a lie like this can even be an omission of facts…so you don't really have to lie at all!"

"What do you mean?"

"There are lots of examples. For instance, Stalin, who caused the murder of millions of rich peasants in his rush to the collective State, became Uncle Joe in the US newsreels when America entered the war and the Soviets were an Allied nation against Hitler, the mass murderer. Other examples are a Chinese warlord who became a democratic reformer, and how the heroic Swiss Army and geography saved the Swiss from occupation during World War II. The fact is that the Swiss became collaborators and offered themselves as a clearinghouse for Nazi spoils of war. You tell the story one way long enough and people will accept it as fact. Today, tormentors become victims of their own past and should be understood and forgiven. And the Allied armies have become in some quarters of history nothing more than political and economic opportunists. How many American business interests are tied to our former enemies of World War II?"

"Come on, Ben! The government is still arresting Nazi war criminals."

"Yes, but most of them are guards or low-level Nazis. None of the men from the higher ranks have been arrested. And those who were have been good American citizens since coming to this country, or so we are told. One former Nazi even became an important international figure, with his link to the Nazi Party explained away as a youthful folly. And when it became apparent that it was much more, he fell back on the 'I was only following orders' argument. He is still an international figure in the United Nations.

"Look at the traitors of the Second World War. If they were not captured and executed in the aftermath of the war, their punishment did not fit their crimes. There is even sympathy for Iva Toquri Aquino, whom we knew as Tokyo Rose. She is now being portrayed as an unfortunate victim of the major political powers of the war. Even better is the idea that dropping the A-bomb was a cruel and inhuman act done for political reasons because the leaders of Japan were ready to give up."

"Yeah, I see what you mean. I had a conversation not too long ago about World War II business interests with my neighbor, a history professor," said CE. "She told me that business has been selling the big lie for years. Standard Oil Company refused to give up patents held by its companies in Germany. When the public reactions became too negative, they rebranded with a red, white, and blue chevron to create a patriotic image. Even drug companies played the patent game. Our troops in the Pacific were denied the use of a substitute quinine pill to prevent malaria. Documents that showed this cooperation between the US and German drug companies were later sold to a stamp dealer in New York, who gave them to the US government—and now these documents have been lost. The list of companies that were working both sides of the war is a who's who of business.

"Even after the war, German companies were still trying to collect money for war damages. The US government paid twenty million dollars in the 1960s for German buildings that were destroyed by US aircraft during the war. Those very same buildings were manufacturing equipment that was sinking our ships supplying the men fighting the Germans. Yet we paid them twenty million dollars for those buildings! And at the same time, Congress refused to grant compensation to Japanese Americans for property and income they lost when they were forced into internment camps during the war. As Alfred Sloan Jr. said, 'International business operates in strictly business terms without regard to political beliefs.'"

"CE, history is history, and all we can do is put the facts together in some context that makes sense."

"Unfortunately, in time we forget the facts," CE said. "And if there is nobody around to remind us, then we seldom remember the way it was then and instead accept new interpretations without question. I think the facts about Mr. Rossmann are coming together, and I do not think people will believe them."

"Let's hear your theory, CE."

"I think that Rossmann and Heidi Miller were part of a German assassination group sent to this country to kill Franklin Delano Roosevelt."

"Wow! What on earth makes you come to that conclusion?"

"Rossmann said in his ramblings that he came by U-boat to kill someone in Georgia. The only person in Georgia important enough for a Nazi death team was FDR."

"You are right, CE, nobody is going to believe this wild idea. But for the sake of passing time, let's say I accept that you are right. Did they get the job done?"

"I do not know. The only record is that FDR died at the Little White House in Georgia of a massive cerebral hemorrhage."

"So how are you going to prove your theory? And do you think it's worth it?"

"Unless, I find some record that will support my theory, I won't be able to prove it. After all, the government isn't going to admit that they allowed our enemies to walk right into the home of the president of the United States and kill him. But there is something about this stamp album I found in an out-of-the-way coin shop that may be the key. And I am beginning to think that my near-miss accident on I-5 was not really an accident at all."

"Do you have any proof or evidence of that?"

"No, but it seems that this album has left a trail of danger and death. The landlord of the lady who had the album ended up falling downstairs and breaking his neck. Then the guy who sold me the album was robbed and murdered the same night. And my house was broken into and my international album—the one that looked just like the album I bought from the dead coin dealer—was stolen while I was away. And then, as I look back, I wonder exactly why that Jaguar decided to speed by at that exact time. He'd been sitting on my back bumper for quite a while…"

"Those are interesting theories, CE," Ben said. "But every one of those things may have a perfectly reasonable explanation."

"I know! I just have a feeling that this album is important. I just don't know why. I think I'll go by my neighbor's house and see if I can find out more."

Chapter 37

Hakenkreuz und Hände—issued September 3, 1945

June 30, 1945—the Ratline in Munich

SS Standartenführer Ernest Hoffmann tossed the Waffen SS uniform into the fire, along with the ID card and papers.

"Hurry, time is of the utmost importance. If we are late, they will not wait. Remember, if we are stopped, you are a refugee heading home," the young businessman said.

"And what do I say if they don't believe my story?"

"Listen! We have been over this a dozen times. The people that are making this possible want you out. The only thing that can screw this up is you. So stop worrying. The papers that I have given you are issued from the Red Cross, stating that you were in a forced labor factory and were injured in a bombing raid back in March. The bandage on your head will allow you to claim that you are suffering from some loss of memory, and the burns on your arm will cover your SS number. So off you go."

"How do I make contact next?" Ernest asked the young man.

"You will be contacted at the proper time when you are in North Africa. Do not worry.

Your expertise will be very valuable in the coming struggle."

"I do not know why you had to destroy Germany when we could have joined forces and marched on the Red Menace together."

"Public opinion, old boy, public opinion! Now get going! We will save the world later. Besides the Red Menace is only a sideshow."

Ernest boarded the train and never looked back.

The younger man looked at the older man standing nearby and asked, "Have we done the right thing?"

"Yes, these guys are bad, but compared to Stalin, they are second rate at best. Hitler killed those he did not like, but Stalin kills anyone. Plus, like Churchill said, he worked with the devil to win the war against the Nazis, and we did win. Now we need to work with the devil's disciples to defeat the political and economic cancer that is infecting the world."

"What do you mean?" the younger man asked.

"Stalin is rushing to win all the knowledge he can for the Soviet Union. So we must find everything first and study what the Germans are working on, or we will lose. Stalin is no dummy. You can bet he is moving troops to the east right now to sweep into China and Japan before we can move in. We need to end the war in the Pacific before Stalin enters. We don't want to share the spoils with him. He has the largest army in the world, and there is no need to provide him with biological, chemical, and technical weapons that we are getting from German and Japanese sources."

"So we are technically breaking the law to protect our future?" the young man asked, sounding slightly confused.

"That's very simply put, but…yes. We have investments to protect and research to do that will save lives. The Russians have taken a beating in this war, and they do not plan to let that happen again. They are not going to go home and wait for the next war. They will put everything into defense and protection. We need to fight by their rules. This is a business issue, and business is the seat of power for all political systems."

"How do we know it's the right thing?"

"Listen, this world is a mess right now and will be for the next few years. The Allied nations argue at every point and mistrust each other, and no one trusts the Russians and they do not trust anybody else. But the war is over, and we have destroyed the war machine of the enemy. Take a gun away from a thug, and you still have a thug. We need these thugs to inform on the other thugs. It is that simple. But enough of that. We have a job to do."

"What's that?"

"There is a Croatian priest that our friend Tito from Yugoslavia would like back. The church would like to keep him in place at his monastery—which is especially interesting because the priest is running a separate ratline.

Chapter 38

Wehrmacht, Artillerie—issued March 21, 1943

April 1945—New York

Charles Moody motioned for his son Rudy to come into the room and sit down. "Rudy, we need you to go to Europe. The whole place is an economic and social mess. There are millions of displaced peoples and refugees, and that number is going to get bigger. The real problem is financial. During the war, the Germans moved gold and other valuables around and even buried some of them. As the war started to go against them, they looted even more on the way out of countries they occupied. Trains headed for Germany with artwork, silverware, jewelry, and anything that had value, including documents.

"That seems to be an Allied command problem. What can I do about it?"

"The problem is that the Allied command is overwhelmed and needs as many experts in as many fields as they can get."

"So, you want me to go over and assist Allied Command? Doing what?"

"Do whatever they need. Just remember some of these people have different interests and loyalty to dangerous political ideas. We want you to protect our interests. When you get to England, our people will be put in touch with individuals on the continent. But be careful. Some of these people have worked behind enemy lines to share our interest."

"You mean spies?"

"Yes, and they have some individuals who need to be brought to this country now, without all the red tape and legal background checks."

"So, again, how do I do this? And why me?"

"You are an associate of our group, and this operation comes from the highest level of government. You are our demonstration of sincerity. Once Hoffmann hears your name, he will relay to his contacts that all is legitimate and the plan can move ahead."

"When do I leave?"

"Tonight. There is a military flight waiting for you as soon as you get to the airport."

Chapter 39

Reich Labor Service Corpsmen—issued June 26, 1943

August 20, 2001, at 7:00 p.m.—shadows of the past

C.E. stopped by to visit his neighbor, a professor of history at a local university. He rang the doorbell, wondering why this album thing had gotten under his skin this deep. The door opened, and Professor Helen Wall smiled broadly when she saw him. "CE, how good to see you! You are never home."

"Hi, Helen. I hope I am not interrupting anything."

"No, no, come in. Can I fix you a drink? I was having a glass of wine and getting ready to watch one of my vices—a Hollywood gossip show."

"I'll have whatever you are having, if it is no trouble."

"No problem! Oh, I can't believe I said that! I hate it when people say that instead of saying 'thank you' or 'you're welcome.'"

"The world is changing."

"Speaking of change, what brings you to my humble home this evening?" the professor said, handing CE a glass of red wine.

CE told her about Heidi and Rossmann and what Rossmann had said about his secret mission. She sat quietly, listening without interrupting him with questions. When he was done, she asked, "So what do you think, CE?"

"I think I'm right. The only person I know of in Georgia who was important enough to have a Nazi hit team sent to kill him was FDR."

"Well, the conspiracy crowd would love to hear your story. The death of every president has had some link to a conspiracy."

"Could these people have been sent to do the job and just got here too late? I mean, suppose they did come to assassinate FDR and he died before they got to Georgia. Why would they stay?"

"Well, they could not book a flight back to Germany right away without arousing suspicion. And if they did go back, they might be recognized. Staying here would most likely be the safest thing to do right after the war."

"Why would here be safer?"

"When the war trials began, many war criminals were sent to other countries to be tried. Many of them escaped through the ratline from Germany to North Africa, where they stayed for awhile before moving to other countries with new identities. It wasn't long before they could leave Germany under their own names, even if they were on the war criminal list."

"You're kidding, I hope!"

"No, I'm sorry to say. War criminals often go unpunished. Both Russia and America brought Nazi scientists into their rocket programs. Of course, the business community saw this as building our technological base, even if it meant breaking our own laws. Some criminals' records were completely erased, as if their part in the war had never happened, if we could use what they had learned through human experimentation during the war, even though their research was done on human beings against their will. It was the Cold War, and any information collected was a leg up on the other side."

The professor continued, "Just to be clear, our government has made an effort in the last twenty years or so to discover Nazi war criminals in this country. It is just hard to find witnesses and paper-work to prove the cases against them."

"Could they still have an organization working in our country?"

"Ah, now you *have* joined the conspiracy mentality group!"

"No, I am just trying to figure out how these people were able to stay in the country for so many years. I mean, Heidi was an SS member with a book filled with some sort of code. And Rossmann was an SS camp guard who was hiding in plain sight in a nursing home, and his doctor disappeared at the exact same time his patient died suddenly and mysteriously. These people were connected, and I want to find out how."

"You think businessmen allowed these individuals to stay in this country?"

"I don't know. You told me the other day about some U.S. companies doing questionable things during the war. You know, Standard Oil and its red, white, and blue rebranding. Were there others?"

The professor paused and then answered, "Many more. And at the heart of it all was the Swiss banking system. Swiss banks are renowned as the best in the world for keeping money safe and protected. Yet after the war, when Jewish relatives were seeking their inheritances from Swiss bank accounts, they were told they had to provide death certificates. That would be very difficult, since most of the claims were filed by relatives who survived the death camps, so they would never receive death certificates. Other bureaucratic roadblocks held the relatives off until the 1990s, when the bankers finally agreed to a settlement, but these settlements were too late for many of the survivors."

"So maybe I can find a business connection in all this?"

"CE, there is always a business connection. So your problem is not to prove a business connection but to show that the connection broke the law—and that is most likely impossible."

"Well, I may be chasing giants, but I need to work on this a little longer. I would appreciate your keeping our conversation quiet for now, if you do not mind. I have a bad feeling about all of this."

"Sure, CE," the professor said with a smile. "Besides, if I told anyone what you just told me, he would say you were nuts—and I would half believe him!"

Chapter 40

Feldpostbeamter—issued March 3, 1944

April 1945—Georgia—Album Cod

There was a knock on the door, followed by a waiter saying, "Room service!"

Steiner went to the door and opened it. The waiter rolled the dinner cart in. "Shall I set this up for dinner, sir?"

"No, we can do that, thank you," Steiner said, handing the waiter a tip. He closed the door as the waiter walked out of the room.

"What are we going to do?" Heidi asked, looking at both men. Rossmann sat quietly, choosing not to respond.

Steiner looked at these two people he had been saddled with. They had been good for the assignment they were sent here for, but now they were just workers with no work. The assignment was terminated, and Steiner and his friends would have to look at long-term arrangements.

"For now, you and Heidi are going back to California. You'll leave on the train tomorrow evening. When you get to San Francisco, the man who met us on the beach road will pick you up, and you will work at his ranch until we have a new assignment or get orders. Do you remember him?"

"Of course," Heidi reassured him.

"At least that dirty American bastard is dead, and we can still win this war," Rossmann said. "I only hope that he suffered as much as he has made Germany suffer by helping the English pigs."

"Rossmann, did you pay attention on the trip across this country? It is full of wealth, man! We ate like kings on the train. And what did we have to eat in Germany? Potatoes. We have lost this war, so we must now wait and plan for the next war."

"Then let's do as much damage we can and make the scum pay a high price."

"This country is large, and I doubt we can damage it given a year."

"We could try," Heidi said optimistically.

"To what end? No, our best option is to wait and plan."

"Okay, but if I can make these arrogant American bastards bleed, I will!"

"No! You will not!" Steiner commanded in his stern, military tone. "Understood?"

Rossmann was so shocked that he immediately came to attention and gave the Nazi salute.

"Rossmann, remember that you are under my command. My first order is to knock off the salute and heel clicking. You are an American, and you'd better blend in and start to love apple pie and baseball. I want you both to listen very closely. Do not draw attention to yourselves. No more accidents with conductors. Do you understand?"

"That conductor was going to make trouble for us."

"Rossmann, that conductor was a fool with no evidence of anything except his nose. You, on the other hand, caused an investigation of his disappearance that could have ended our mission. I do not want any more stunts. You are to do nothing without my permission. Understood?"

Yes, we act normal and do nothing to draw attention to ourselves.

Chapter 41

**Order of Prince Alexander Nevski—
issued May 30, 1940**

Overprint 1945

September 1946—business is business

The room on the twenty-second floor was small and narrow, and the men in it sat around a long hand-carved, mahogany table. They belonged to various business organizations, but they were not representing those businesses today. This group of like-minded men felt that the world needed saving—and only they could save it. Within their ranks, money was shifted from one place to another to support or protect common interests in the betterment of business and to keep communism at bay.

Vito Carbo sat at one end of the table. "Gentlemen, Mr. Moody thinks our interests would be best served by funding the campaigns of anticommunist politicians, and I agree."

"Reestablishing our business connections in the defeated areas is a paramount concern. The best way to see that all parties work together is to have a common enemy. The meetings at Bretton Woods, Yalta, and Potsdam have shown that Stalin distrusted the West and has his own plans for Europe. The communists are and have been our common enemy," Moody said with a smile.

The man to his left said, "And how do you perceive a common enemy will advance our interests?

"The war is over, and your contracts are done—no more defense spending. Yet with the threat of a new enemy that is just as strong or stronger, new contracts will be the first item of business," Moody explained. "Defense and business will come together in a united front against the Red Threat just as they did after the Great War in the 1920s. All we need is a few political candidates to show how far the country has moved to the left, and that is a threat to the nation security."

"How do you plan on getting the candidates?" another man asked.

"The beauty of it is that we do not have to. They are already out there, and they are using anything they can to win elections. Red baiting is being used in a dozen political campaigns as I speak. We just have to funnel funds into those campaigns. As good old Calvin

Coolidge said, 'The business of America is business.' I say, the business of the world is business as usual."

"What about my country?" asked a man from Argentina. "My country does not have a large defense industry, and our major export is beef. So what interest do we have?"

"I would think that answer is fairly obvious," Rudy Moore responded. He glanced down at his watch. He had told his wife, Gladys, that he would be home for dinner. "Your government is worried more about the communist element than ours. They have taken some extraordinary steps to control the socialist influences in the country, including allowing of a significant number of recent changes to the immigration status of German citizens to your country."

"Industry and defense are the key to all our problems in the near future," a French banker asserted. "I will agree with you, but in the 1920s, the business and industrial complex took a beating by the liberals. How will we prevent that same reaction today?"

"To put it in simplistic terms, that has already been done for us," Rudy explained. "At the end of the Great War, there was no real threat to the world power structure. Jobs moved workers away from radical causes and into the middle class. It was only during the Great Depression that the communists started to become a major issue once more. Industry and defense will be seen as the defenders of the Free World and not as the exploiters and merchants of death as they were in the 1920s."

"You make a good point, Rudy," said Charles.

"Yes, but the radicals are better organized now, and we need to keep pressure on them to keep them in line," Rudy said. "Conformity, gentlemen, is the name of the game, and we make the rules. Now I make a motion to adjourn, so let's vote and go have some fun. I think we have the beginnings of a secure future for our enterprise."

Chapter 42

Baseball Centennial—issued June 12, 1939

Franklin Delano Roosevelt expressed a wish that every boy could have a first-day cover. As was the custom, FDR received the first ceremonial cover, which was signed by the postmaster and baseball greats Babe Ruth, Ty Cobb, Cy Young, and others. When some young baseball fans requested this stamp celebrating America's pastime but forgot to include the three cents, the postmaster of Cooperstown paid the missing cost himself so that no boy would be disappointed.

New York, Central Park, 1991

Two men walked toward the Metropolitan Museum.

"Have our contacts in eastern Europe reached out to the Russian elite? They may be falling apart, but we have only lost part of an old enemy. China and North Korea are still communists and a threat. Plus, since the oil crisis of 1974, the Middle East is a concern. They will do something to pull us into a protective mode," the taller man said.

"How do we use that to help us?"

"Money is the key. For example, Saudi Arabia is the largest oil producer in the world. The only other real commodity they have is sand. That means they have to import food. They have leverage with oil, and we have leverage with food. They will need our expertise in oil production and related industries to keep production rates up, and they will make the price of oil high enough to keep the market stable. Now the Saudis know they have a weak spot in food production, so they will need our expertise in new methods of food production—and we will keep the price high enough to keep the market stable."

"I can see that there is codependence. But how is that related to our situation in defense and international business today?" the shorter man asked.

"Business has always been international. It was international business that sent Marco Polo east and Columbus west," the taller man explained. "No empire or state expanded without a business connection. Behind every religious, philosophical, or political movement, there was always money. Adam Smith used business to explain the benefits of capitalism, and Karl Marx used it to explain the natural evolution of society. However, it was Mussolini who pulled business into the open with his corporate state of fascism in the 1920s. Today, the corporate state is global. The global economy is so interlocked that national markets can collapse as global corporations become stronger."

The shorter man gave the taller man a confused look.

"Take, for example, the auto industry. In the 1920s, the industry was made up by over 100 of different auto companies. But, by the 1960s, there were only the big three and they were diversified into other industries. Then the Japanese auto industries entered the American market. Who do you think provided the money for the Japanese auto industry to expand? It expanded into the small car market at first and Americans were still buying big and fast cars. So the American car manufactures did not worry. By the 1970s the Japanese cars were taking a larger share of the market. They asked women what they wanted in a car. They made sports cars with automatic gear shifts and cup holders. They put a mirror on the sun visor on the driver's side."

The shorter man still looked confused. "Who put up the money?"

"A large part of it came from the American auto industry for a share of the profits in smaller cars. Only they did not see that the Japanese would expand into all types of cars, and the American industry was hurting by the 1970s."

"Then what about the German cars?"

"Look at World War II," the taller man explained. "The Volkswagen, known in Germany as the People's Wagon, was the brainchild of Hitler and his Nazi bureaucrats. The only reason it didn't take off sooner is because production was stopped during the war so the factories could make tanks. Then after the war and within a few years, German industry was producing them again with the help of the British and American governments to build up the economy to control the communist threat. The first VW sold in America was cheap with no heater or radio. In time, larger and full-equipped models were being exported to the United States. Both the Japanese and German car companies are now building their cars in this country. We just have to stay behind the scenes and wait. You see, as businessmen, we make decisions on cost analysis, not national interest or pride."

"That's a little cold-blooded, don't you think?"

"Not at all! Business is beneficial to mankind. It has provided almost every improvement in our lives and our lifestyles. When we leave change to governments, they exploit the lives of their citizens and conquer in the name of power. But business conquests are much cleaner—and only the strong survive."

Zimmermann SS54682

Chapter 43

Wehrmacht Series: Kradfahrer—issued March 21, 1943

August 23, 2001—University Library

CE was sitting with Professor Archibald Billings Cummings, commonly known as Professor ABC, in the university library.

"You and Professor Wall gave me a startle when you came knocking on my door at ten p.m. last night. News is rarely good at that time of night. Then you told me this incredible story that piqued my interest. So tell me more!"

CE pulled out his stamp album and opened it to a page with four stamps and the name Miller followed by SS12306.

"Helen's area of expertise is economics, so we have pieced that together somewhat. But we hope you may be able to tie it together with your knowledge of twentieth-century European history," CE said.

"This is not a lot of information to start with, CE What else can you tell me about this Miller person?" the professor asked. He opened his laptop and logged in.

"Her name was Heidi Miller, and she had lived in Oroville, California, since December 1945. Before that, she worked on a ranch in northern California as a cook. I could not find any record of her before 1945."

"Well, let me see if we can find a social security number for our old girl. Then I will go into some of the networks with information on the Nazis and try to find her number there."

"When you go into those Nazi files, I have another name and number for Dr. Claus Zimmermann," CE said, turning to the Zimmermann page in the album. "He was the doctor who was looking after the SS man, Rossmann, at the rest home in Oroville."

"What was Rossmann's number? I might as well look it up at the same time."

"Here it is, Eric Wolfgang Rossmann, number SS375082."

"This will take a bit of time, so let me work at it. I'll call you when I get something."

"Thanks, Professor! I appreciate your help."

"Glad to," the professor responded. "This is real history. Sometimes it fills in the blanks, and other times it opens more questions—and I love a good mystery."

Chapter 44

Volkssturn Angehörige Adler—issued January 1945

September 1, 2001—Professor ABC's office

"I got your call and came over as fast as I could," said CE.

"I'm glad you did! If that book you have is what I think it is, you have uncovered a list of Nazi military and businessmen that have been living in this country for years. I did some digging into the old Nazi files and found a Heidi Miller who was a member of the staff at a camp in Poland. After a little more digging, I found her as a member of the Hitler Youth."

"How can you be sure it's the same Heidi Miller?" asked CE.

"That is the best part. It seems that this Heidi Miller, SS12306, was born in Germantown, Pennsylvania, in 1922. The record I found in Hitler Youth said her father was a party official, and she was allowed in the youth because of his rank. Yet there was still suspicion of her loyalty to the Fatherland. Plus, your Heidi Miller applied for a social security card using her Germantown birth certificate, but she didn't do so until 1945."

"That's good information," CE said, "but it's all very circumstantial. We can't go to the authorities without more."

"Every name and number you gave me from the stamp album is connected to the Nazis in either the military or the business world. The stamps on the individual pages give us their names, the years they entered the country, the transportation they used, and the organizations they belonged to in Germany."

"That is unbelievable! What do we do now?"

"I have a friend in the US State Department. I will call and set up an appointment. My contact is a woman I used to date, so we can trust her. And just so you know, I dated her in college," the professor chuckled. "I don't want you to get the idea that there was any kind of professor-student relationship going on."

"The thought would never cross my mind. I hear your class is so easy no one would ever have to sleep with you to pass. And besides, you aren't good looking enough to get a date at a bar at two a.m., much less an attractive younger woman."

The professor chuckled again. "I'll tell my wife she really needs to rethink her taste in men!"

"Let's not bring her into it! She's definitely your better half! I would never want to offend her!"

"Too late, my friend! My bad taste in men have continued with the present company." The professor's wife stepped into the room.

CE got up and gave her a hug. "I'll be on my way and will mend my ways."

"I'll call when I get anything."

"Great, you two take care."

Chapter 45

Four Freedoms—issued February 12, 1943

This stamp commemorated the "Four Freedoms" speech Franklin Delano Roosevelt made to encourage the nation away from isolationism and toward providing assistance to Great Britain.

September 2, 2001—Federal Building in Los Angeles, California

"Good afternoon. I'm Special Agent Albert Morgan. How may I help you two gentlemen?" said the agent behind the desk.

"My name is CE Hall, and this is Professor Archibald B. Cummings. We have an appointment."

"Yes, I was told that you have information on war criminals and a secret organization working in this country."

CE pulled the stamp album out and placed it on the desk. Then he blurted out the whole story of his discovery. He spoke quickly, trying not to leave out any details. He talked about the Nazis, the business entanglements, the political maneuvering, even the murders. Then he stopped for a breath.

"That is quite a story! It seems mostly circumstantial, but you have piqued my interest," the agent said. "As you know, pursuing war criminals is my specialty, though the ones I have sought out so far are from Eastern Europe and Central America. I've never located any from before 1980. So this could be a real challenge…"

"It seems to me that the best path may be to follow the money," Professor Cummings said. "These people did not get into this country without help. Now that help had to be very well connected with power and money."

CE interrupted him. "Yes, this is a sensitive issue that could cause embarrassment for some pretty important people. Our own government may have even been complicit."

"I just can't believe the government is behind this," Agent Morgan said. "You're starting to sound like a conspiracy theorist."

"I'm not saying they invited this mass invasion. But our government did bring some Nazis into the country by less-than-legal methods in the period right after the war, all for the cause of national security. How far would our rocket program have been without the help of Nazi scientists? Then there were all those ex-Nazis who helped us find out what the Russians were up to behind the Iron Curtain. Let's face it—the Cold War gave us some strange bedfellows."

Agent Morgan shook his head. "Still, you can't possibly think that our own government engaged a Nazi hit team to kill the president! It's a little too incredible, don't you think?"

"Then prove us wrong," CE said. "We only have so much access to information on the internet. You, on the other hand, can use the resources of the US government to dig a little deeper."

"I have to admit, I am curious. So let me have the album for a couple of days, and I'll get back to you."

"That is not possible. This album is too valuable. And I've already lost a similar album to the men I believe are looking for it," CE said. "But I'll let you photocopy the pages, and I'll give you this written record of events and names from my research."

"Sounds good. But I cannot promise anything."

CE nodded. "I understand. And one other thing...please don't tell anyone about this story or why you are looking into Nazi war criminals. We don't know who we can trust. We only came to you only because we think you're too young to be involved."

"Then I would say you two did not think this through very well!"

"Why do you say that?" asked the professor.

"If this book is still important as you think it is, then whoever is connected to it has to be generational. We could be going on the third generation of Nazi spies in the U.S., gentlemen!"

"Why do you think I will not allow this album to leave my side, Agent Morgan?"

"It's good to know that it's not personal. You clearly have trust issues with everyone!"

"No just individuals that want to harm the country."

Chapter 46

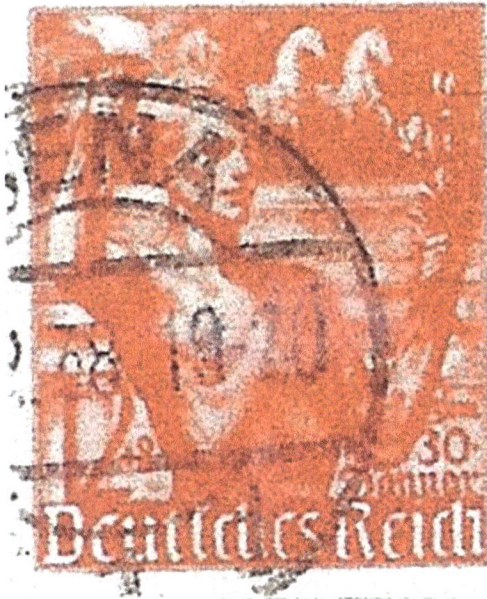

Fackelträger vor dem Brandenburger
tor—issued January 28, 1938

September 4, 2000—the Wall Street Office of Rudy C. Moody

"What are we going to do NOW?" Congressman Chase said, his voice escalating to a very high pitch.

He was sitting across the table from Rudy Moody in a large room overlooking the World Trade Center towers. Ernest Hoffman sat to his left, and on the other side were William Steiner and Dr. Claus Zimmermann.

"Calm down, Robert!" Rudy said impatiently. "Let's look at the situation and then make a calculated plan of action. We are not the first group to find they have a critical problem."

"Yeah, that's easy for you to say," the congressman grumbled. "You can hide behind your corporation and subsidiaries around the world. I am a congressman in front of the public every day. Every move I make is watched, and every word I say is heard and remembered. These people are like sharks! When they smell blood, I'll be the one they circle. So don't tell me to calm down, Rudy!"

Steiner frowned. "Listen, you two, I have been at this longer than the two of you put together. Turning on each other is not going to solve the problem. So instead of tearing each other up, let's try to find out the extent of the problem."

"You're right, William," said Rudy. "Where do we start?"

"Suppose we start with Zimmermann," Steiner said, tilting his head toward the man sitting next to him.

"I was heading to the airport when I heard on the radio that there was a Nazi at the rest home in Oroville posing as a Jewish Holocaust survivor. The guy on the radio said that an insurance investigator had come to the rest home to ask Mr. Rossmann some questions and ended up telling the staff that Rossmann was in the SS. As soon as I heard the news, I turned around immediately and headed for the rest home. As the midnight shift began, I snuck into Rossmann's room and took care of the problem."

"Do you think that was smart, doctor?" asked Robert.

"It seemed the best solution. Rossmann had lost control. We couldn't have him spouting things about missions and killings. And I was careful. The medication I used to remove him was from the cabinets at the hospital, and I took the empty vials with me. So at least that part of this little problem has been taken care of."

"Let's not jump to conclusions. We don't know how much that insurance investigator knows. He could have stumbled across Rossmann. We won't be in serious trouble unless he is able to decipher the code in the stamp album. Then we'll need to act quickly. What have you got, Ernst?"

"Just to be safe, we followed the insurance inspector," Ernst said. "I could tell from his conversation with the guy in the coroner's office and his professor friend that he was starting to figure things out. So I arranged a little accident."

"How did that work out, Ernest?" Robert said sarcastically.

"Robert, if you cannot be civil, please do not enter into the conversation," Rudy said firmly. "We are trying to get the facts together, not place blame. Ernst, please continue."

"It seemed like a perfect plan. If everything had gone as planned, his car would have tumbled into the road in oncoming traffic—and we wouldn't have had to worry about him anymore. But he's either really good or really lucky."

The congressman interrupted. "It's not just the insurance inspector we have to worry about. I have had my staff looking into war crimes in Kosovo so I can see who's poking around in the war crimes files. It seems that there is someone in intelligence looking at Nazi war crimes in the US. In fact, they're searching for Zimmermann, Miller, Steiner, and Hoffmann. Connections will be made soon, and they could be linked to our organization!"

Rudy held his hand up to calm the congressman before his voice reached the heightened pitch. "Let's look at this situation a little closer and meet again in two days. Then we'll make a plan."

Hoffmann

Chapter 47

Brandenburger tor mit Reichsadler—
issued January 26, 1943

September 1946—A Train Station in Rome

The train pulled into the station after a long journey. War damage and the mass of displaced people moving from one location in Europe to another made travel slower and more difficult than it once had been. Ernest Hoffmann got off the train and walked toward the front of the station.

"Mr. Hoffmann?" asked a US Army sergeant.

"Yes?"

"Sir, if you will follow me."

"What is this about?"

"Sir, my orders are to pick you up and deliver you to a ship at the port. That is all I know. May I help you with your bags, sir?"

"Yes, Thank you. Can you tell me who sent you?"

"Sir, I am so far down the food chain that by the time I know anything it's already happened. One minute I'm sitting at my desk, and the next thing a guy in civilian clothes comes into the office and starts giving orders to a general. They handed me this photo of you and these papers and told me to give you everything when I put you on the ship."

"Then I guess we'd better get going, Sergeant."

"My Jeep is over to the right. I could not get a staff car at such a late notice."

"That's all right, a Jeep will probably be faster. Mussolini may have gotten the Italian trains running on time, but Italian road work leaves something to be desired."

On the ride to the port, Ernest remembered the first time he was in Rome. His father, Werner Hoffmann, had banking and business contacts in the Italian government and had taken Ernest to Rome before the war started. That trip had ensured Ernst's future—for the war and beyond.

"How long have you been in the service?" Hoffmann asked, passing the time.

"Three years," the sergeant answered. "And I'd just as soon forget it all. As soon as I can, I'm going home so I can forget this whole mess and enjoy life on my family farm. Here we are at your ship, sir. Have a good trip."

"Thank you, Sergeant," Hoffmann said. Then he got out of the car and walked up the ramp and onto the ship.

On board, Hoffmann was introduced to the captain and shown to his private cabin. Once inside, he opened the envelope the sergeant had given him.

Inside was a list of contact names in Egypt. There was also a summary of a meeting that was held in July 1944 at a place called Bretton Woods. When Hoffmann finished reading the documents, he took out a match and burned them. As he watched the pages burn, he frowned as he considered what he had learned. Allied powers were already restructuring the world financial system before the end of the war. They had set up the World Bank and International Monetary Fund to control the flow of money for the long term, while the people of influence in Germany had stolen everything they could get their hands on.

When the pages were nothing but ashes, Hoffmann wrapped them in a towel, took them out on deck, and let the breeze blow the ashes away. Then he went to have dinner with the captain and crew.

The meal was served at a table large enough for twelve diners. There was an orange tablecloth and ten settings of flatware. Hoffmann sat at the only seat not taken, which was beside the captain.

"I am sorry to offer you only spaghetti and meatballs tonight," the captain said.

"Spaghetti is wonderful! I have not eaten so well since the Allied troops entered the factory where I was a forced laborer. I have grown accustomed to the rich foods of the West, and it is beginning to show." He patted his stomach and smiled.

"You will enjoy the food in Egypt as well, sir. What is the reason for your visit? Do you have family there?" the captain asked.

"Yes," Hoffmann said. "My late wife's sister lives there with her husband. She was lucky and escaped Germany in 1933. Unfortunately, I thought that things would get better and stayed until it was too late. Because of my political views, I was sent to a concentration camp and eventually put to work as a forced laborer in an aircraft plant. When the factory was bombed, I was seriously injured, but the American doctors performed small miracles with my wounds, but I still have some memory loss. As you can see, I still have a bandage for my head injury and some burn scars."

"What were your political views that upset the Nazis so much, if I may ask?"

"I really do not know. All that I can remember is that I was a social democrat and made the mistake of telling the Nazis that the move to single party rule was wrong for Germany. In the early hours of the next morning, I was awakened and taken to a concentration camp. It was brutal, even barbaric."

"Well, Mr. Hoffmann, you are lucky to have lived through it and should be grateful to have lost some of your memory."

"That may be true, but the part I remember is difficult to live with."

After dinner, the captain went to his cabin to find a man sitting in his room. "What do you think?" the man asked with an English accent.

"He played his part well, and his answers were, how shall I say, touching," the captain said.

"Good! Then we can make arrangements to send him to the U.S. quickly. His knowledge of banking in the occupied territories will help with the rebuilding of Europe and help us avoid the Soviet link. The Red Army is packing everything they can and moving it east. There is a joke going around Berlin that the Soviets are ripping up toilet bowls and sending them home as potato washers. Can you imagine that?"

"That is funny, and yes, I can. I did some work at the U.S. Embassy in Moscow in 1940, and the living conditions for people outside of Moscow were bad—and that's the places I was allowed to go. I can't imagine what it was like in the places I wasn't allowed to travel!" The captain shook his head sadly.

The English man nodded his assent. "All I know is that the Red Army is not reducing its troop commitments in eastern Europe. Every day the tensions between the Russians and Europe are getting worse. They push, and we retaliate. They have actively tried to move their political appointees into government positions. Trust me when I say that Berlin is going to be a problem for a long time, but it is a good place to keep an eye on Joe and the boys."

"And that's why we need to work with guys like Hoffmann. We are not here to judge character. If we were, most of the network we are building would have been removed from consideration."

"It's the lesser of two evils, I know. To the Russians, Stalin is a genius and a great leader, while we see him as a ruthless politician wanting to expand his political power. If he gives anything, it is because he has something bigger planned. As much as I distrust Hoffmann, I distrust the Soviets more."

Chapter 48

Argentina Industry—issued October 31, 1946

August 1946—Argentina

"Mr. Hoffmann, I hope you enjoy your flight to New York City," the stewardess said, smiling and offering him a hot towel. An attractive red head with long legs, she filled out her uniform very nicely. Hoffmann's admiring gaze conveyed his appreciation for her beauty. She had been flying this route for two months, and it was not the first time a man had looked at her in this way. The flight was a highly desired route for stewardesses because the businessmen that traveled it were young and moving up in the world. It was a good hunting ground for a successful husband.

"I'm sure I will, thanks to you," Hoffmann said with a smile.

"If there is anything you need, just let me know. We will be taking off in a few moments." Ernest smiled again at the stewardess just as a voice came over the intercom.

"This is your captain speaking. The flight crew and I hope to make your travel on American Airlines as comfortable as we can. Thank you for choosing American Airlines for your travel needs."

Ernest Hoffmann closed his eyes and thought about his life, finally dozing off as the engines roared toward America.

Chapter 49

**Adler im Kampf mit Schlangen—
Issued November 9, 1944**

February 1940—the office of
Reichsführer Heinrich Himmler

Reichsführer Heinrich Himmler, Reich Marshall Hermann Goering, and Reich Minister and official of the Reich Bank Werner Hoffmann were all present when the meeting started.

"Gentlemen, let's begin," Hermann Goering said. "There will be no notes taken, and our actions must be completed while Stalin is still our friend." A low laugh from the others followed his last statement.

"I have been invited to address the government's concern of financial resources," Hoffmann said. "The simple fact is that we do not have enough gold in reserve to support a prolonged war effort."

"You bankers said that last time and still got rich while we died at the front," said Goering.

"What you say is true to some degree, Reich Marshall. However, money was not the reason we lost the last time," Hoffmann said. "This time money will be all the more important for resources and technology advancements."

"So, what is your plan to prevent this financial problem from happening?" asked Himmler.

"Quite simple, we take charge of the banks in the countries we conquer and work with the neutral countries that we can for cash flow," Hoffmann explained.

"What?" the two other men said in unison.

"We need cash to buy resources from neutral parties. If that money comes from a neutral party, it will be easier to purchase what we need. With the restrictions placed on trade with America, we need to find places our cash will open doors."

"How do you plan on doing this?"

"We are already doing it," Hoffmann said with a smug grin. "Since coming to power, each of you has become rich. You are living in big homes with country estates, and your wealth is the means by which we can succeed."

"What are you implying, Ernest?" asked Josef with a menacing undertone in his voice.

"All I mean is that each of you has made contacts with foreign bankers, and those contacts have been lucrative for everyone involved. We can move money all over the world with those connections. And when we are done, we will be the only ones who know where the funds are—and we can make them available for the Reich."

The rest of the men nodded their agreement.

"I have just one question, Werner," Josef asked. "Who will handle those contacts?"

"My son Ernst has contacts in Eastern Europe, the Americas, and the Middle East. No one in the world can match his understanding of the international banking world. And he is a virtually unknown figure. He is perfect for the job."

"That sounds like it will work out better for you than it will for the rest of us," Hermann said.

"His expertise will be invaluable to our operation, Hermann," Hoffmann said. "Let me give you an example. In the Middle East, religious beliefs forbid a person to give loans that collect interest."

"So! How do the banks make money?" Hermann asked.

"Gifts equal to the amount of interest. That satisfies the restriction, and both parties get what they want. It is a matter of understanding the culture you are working in. That is where Ernst comes in. He has extensive knowledge of world cultures and national attitudes."

"Then we have a go, comrades!" said Himmler.

Chapter 50

Posthorn und Brief—issued October 2, 1944

April 1945 at 5:00 a.m.—gold train in the Bavarian Mountains

The train was making its way through the mountains of Bavaria at what many believed would be the last stand of the German Reich. It was Hitler's last battle or his greatest victory, depending on which side you were on. Ernst Hoffmann had no illusions of victory. His plan was to bury the gold on the train and wait until he could use it.

Sitting on the train gave him time to wonder how these fools got as far as they did. Reich Marshall Goering was an egotistical drug addict, whom Ernst had to admit was the smartest of the group. Reichsführer Himmler was a short man with a Napoleon complex and a cruel personality. Yet he was so weak that he could not watch his own murderous acts carried out.

Ernst remembered how on one visit to a death camp, Himmler had vomited all over his shoes when he saw a Jewish woman shot in the head. However, Himmler could be manipulated with greed. As a matter of fact, so could Goering.

Goebbels, on the other hand, was the most dangerous of the trio. He was the fanatic believer, and so was his Hitler-loving wife. This whole train trip was Goebbels's plan to fight to the very end. But Goebbels had committed suicide and killed his family rather than live without Hitler.

Ernst was thinking of his orders to travel only at night. Only a fool would try to move a train in daylight with the air over the route under the control of Allied forces. Goering's Air Force had not been a factor for the last year, even with the new super weapon, the jet fighter. It might have made an impact if Hitler had not changed the production orders from jet fighter to jet bomber and then back to jet fighter, wasting valuable production time. Hitler was a great war leader, but he was so afraid of upsetting German women that he produced lipstick until 1944 when the German Army desperately needed bullets. When all was said and done, German defeat could be laid at Hitler's feet.

Ernst's reminiscing was interrupted by a soldier calling his name.

"Herr Hoffmann! Herr Hoffmann! The track is damaged, and we need to replace some rails."

"How long will it take?"

"A couple of hours at the least."

"Then get started. I do not want to be caught in the open by an Allied aircraft."

"Yes, sir!" the soldier saluted and ran off to form a work party.

Ernst watched the young man run off and thought, *They are so young.*

Chapter 51

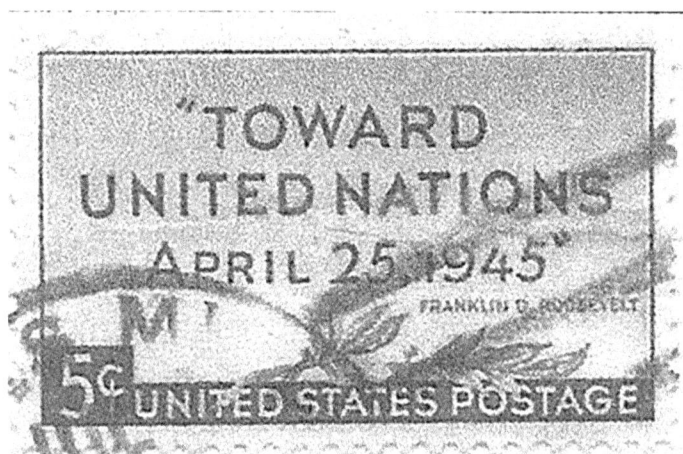

United Nation Conference—issued April 25, 1945

Franklin Delano Roosevelt wanted to avoid repeating the mistakes that occurred at the end of World War I. He believed the conference held in San Francisco should have special recognition. So on April 12, 1945, FDR told his secretary, William D. Hassett, he would purchase the first UN stamps. Within half an hour, the president had a seizure and died.

April 1945 at 9:10 a.m.—Bavarian Mountains

"Sir, there is a train stopped on the tracks just around the bend. They are working on the track." The lieutenant was fresh out of the University of Texas A&M. The shortage of officers had given college graduates the opportunity to gain officer status in the military in the ninety-day officer preparation school. These officers were called ninety-day wonders, and they often had little military experience. The lieutenant had been an economics major in school before he entered the Army.

"Sergeant, take a squad up that hill on the right, and we will hit them at 0930. Got it?" The sergeant was from Louisiana just outside New Orleans. He had been in the war since North Africa and saw his mission as keeping this lieutenant alive, along with the rest of his unit. Thankfully, the lieutenant listened to advice.

"They may have the track fixed by then, sir. It looks like they are almost done."

"Then improvise, Sergeant. Just don't let that train move."

"Yes, sir." The sergeant turned toward his squad and said, "All right, you sorry excuses for soldiers, follow me."

"Sergeant, they're loading up and getting ready to move out down there."

"We're going to have to get down there. Bring that bazooka over here."

Suddenly, the sky was filled with fighters strafing and bombing the tracks. Germans were jumping out of the cars and rushing into the forest for cover. The roar of the P38s and the explosions were deafening. Then, just as fast as the firefight started, the fighters were gone, leaving the train with little damage. The track in front of the train, however, was gone. Slowly, the German troops emerged from the forest and milled around the engine. And at that minute, the U.S. squad hit them, and the lieutenant and the rest of the platoon appeared at the front of the train. The Germans did not even try to fight back.

"Where is your officer?" yelled the sergeant.

One of the Germans pointed to the ground, where Werner Hoffmann lay with blood covering his head. The lieutenant walked over to the body and called the medic.

"Is he dead?" the lieutenant asked the medic.

"No, something hit him. Could have been a bomb fragment during that strafing run. But these guys do not seem to like him much. They put their hands up almost before our first shot."

"Okay, Sergeant, have the Germans pick him up and send the rest of them back to their company. You and I will stay here and see what we've got on this train."

Just then, a soldier called out from one of the freight cars. "Lieutenant, I think you'd better come and look at this."

Chapter 52

Graf Anton Günther—issued January 6, 1945

June 21, 1945—PWO camp interrogation room 23

Ernest Hoffmann sat in the room with two intelligence officers. The one in charge was a British officer, and the other was a young officer from the U.S. Army. Both men had been asking the same questions for seven days, and Ernst had answered every question over and over again. The questions centered on where was the train going. Ernst always gave the same answer—he only knew the town where the trucks would meet the train. Where they went after that he could only guess.

"Let's go over this again. What was your train loaded with, Herr Hoffmann?"

"I am an officer in the German Army. You will address me by my rank."

"You were in the German SS, not the German Army, and you are now our prisoner, Herr Hoffmann. You were caught with stolen property, and some of it can be traced to murdered individuals. So right now, you are nothing but a common criminal. It would be in your best interest to cooperate, or you will find yourself at Nuremberg with the rest of the war criminals," the American officer said.

The officer continued. "But you do have options. It may seem that the war is over, but good old Uncle Joe is not going to play nice. We need to get people we can trust into the Soviet zone. We would like your help in doing that. Your ability to withstand questioning and your connection to the SS and the Nazi Party will be beneficial in helping us to recruit agents. You also have knowledge about the banking system, and we need help tracing the Nazi system."

"What do I get out of this, if I may ask?" Hoffmann asked.

"Helping us is the only way you can help yourself, Herr Hoffmann," the officer said. "When I walk out of this room, your name will be placed on the war criminal list, and you will be sent to a detention center for war criminals. Or you can help us recruit agents who will keep watch on Uncle Joe and you can continue your life," the British officer explained.

"How will you do that?" Hoffmann asked.

"That is my problem and his," the British officer said, pointing toward the American officer. "We need you, and you need us—and right now, you need us a lot more than we need you. So I'm going to walk through that door. And if I shut the door, you are going to be sorry you let that happen."

The British officer pushed his chair back and stood up. Then he looked at the other officer and said, "Coming, Rudy?"

As the British officer put his hand on the doorknob, Hoffmann called out, "Wait! I'll do it!"

Chapter 53

Airplane over Giza Pyramids—issued 1933–1938

Overprint 1946

June 29, 1945—an office in the Bank of Egypt

"Mr. Hoffmann, it is so good to see you again. I see that the cat lands on its feet," said Adli, a tall dark, olive-skinned man with a long thin nose. He smiled brightly as he held his hand out for Ernst Hoffmann to take. "How is your father?"

"It is good to see you again too, Adli," Hoffmann responded. "The last time we met, things were different. And yes, my father is fine. He was able to get out of Berlin before the Russians closed it off."

"Yes, indeed, it was different then. You were winning, and those of us who wanted to rid the Middle East of British and French imperialism saw you as a good weapon against them. But as you can see now, you were not the victors, so we must continue working with the Imperialists. Oh well, time is on our side in these matters."

"As if you ever stopped working with them!" Hoffmann scoffed.

"One must do what one needs to do to achieve one's goals, no? Besides, you are not the one to complain about playing both sides. Your leader signed a deal with Stalin and then both proceeded to cut Poland as the spoils of diplomacy."

"I am not implying anything, Adli. Everyone knew the score, and everyone believed that he would be the last one standing. When things did not work out, it was back to the drawing board to set new objectives to reach our goals."

"What would those objectives and goals be, Ernst?"

"Power and money, Adli! Power and money."

"And what can I do to help you reach that goal, friend?"

"The network we had before the war is still in place and still has the same goals. There are those that want to weaken the control of talented individuals and good business to establish the socialist goals of Stalin. The extreme right in the Middle East wants to destroy the West and anyone who thinks like a Westerner."

"You confuse nationalism with anti-Western culture," Adli corrected.

"No, you need to watch Wahhabism. This group has interpreted the Koran so that a Muslim can kill anyone who is not a true follower—and that includes other Muslims."

"We can handle our radicals," Adli said.

"That is what we said in Germany—and look at what it cost us."

"So what do you propose?"

"There are many new parts to fit into the old parts. But good business is good business. When it comes to national identification, good business comes first."

"What are these new parts?" Adli asked.

"The Soviet Union, for one, and in time, they will want more and more of the Western lifestyle. We will see to it that they want it. The desire to have what one desires is strong in human nature. That promise is like light to a moth for humans."

"I see no reason to end our relationship, my friend."

"I am glad we can continue to work together, Adli," Hoffmann said. "Now I am off to Argentina to talk with some old friends. I will be in touch."

Chapter 54

Adolf Hitler—issued April 13, 1943

August 1946—at the monument of General Jose de San Martin

"Here are your passport and identification papers, Mr. Hoffmann. We have scheduled a direct flight to New York, and there will be no problems. You are now an American citizen returning from a banking business trip to Buenos Aires. Your memory was lost due to the injury to your head during the war, so you will not have any memory before August of 1945 except what you have been told, and that will be vague," said Rudy. "Any questions?"

"No, I think we have covered everything," Hoffmann said. "I am just amazed that your government is part of this operation."

"That is where you are wrong, Ernst. The government is trying to fight the spread of communism, and they will use any means necessary to defeat it! We, on the other hand, want international business to run smoothly without costly glitches. Now if money can be made by a little war now and then, fine. That is good for business. But without the communists, our ability to sell arms would be limited to small players that have only a few dollars to spend on weapons—like the ones you just help to sell to President Peron."

"Then the government knows nothing about this?"

"Let's just say they know you are an anticommunist asset who can work wonders with Eastern European banking and industrial interests. Plus, they are willing to forget your past. We have helped to bring into the country many scientists, engineers, and medical personnel, and the information they provide will help to keep us ahead of the communists."

"So I am now an American banker with international connections with your father's banking firm, correct?"

"Yes—and when you get to New York, you will be introduced as the newest member of the board of directors. You will meet a select few of our clients and members of the organization. By the way, how did you find Argentina?"

"Surprisingly, I saw many old acquaintances."

"Yes, Juan Peron is very open to the funds that your old friends bring. We know the communists are here, and Juan is important to our plans to keep the Reds from gaining control in Latin America. The only problem is that Juan often allows his hunger for power to cause him to actually believe the promises made by others."

Hoffman gave him an inquisitive look.

Rudy continued. "Atomic energy is a complex issue, and Juan believes he has an answer. He is setting his course on a house of straw, and it will be his ruin in the near future, for he has placed his chips on a man who knows little yet makes large plans."

"You have not warned him?"

"No! In the long term, the balance of power in South America would change. So when Juan can help us, let him. The rest of the time, he is free to do what he wants, as long as it does not interfere with our plans. Enjoy your trip, Mr. Hoffmann!"

Chapter 55

Telegraph Centenary—issued May 24, 1944

The daughter of Samuel F.B. Morse called Franklin Delano Roosevelt and asked that the stamp be printed to recognize the telegraph's wartime accomplishments. The president approved the stamp over the objections of Postmaster General Walker.

September 6, 2000, at 5:00 p.m.—Rudy's office

"What are we going to do?" asked Congressman Chase.

"We need to find out what this guy Hall knows and then take some measures to neutralize the damage. But we need to have a plan so we won't repeat the mistakes that have been made already," said Rudy.

"How will we find out what he knows?" asked Werner Hoffmann.

"Follow him and watch. Where he goes, you go. We can piece together a snapshot of what he is doing from his movements. Plus, we have spent a lot of money on electric surveillance equipment, so you should be able to hear most of his conversations. Just do not get noticed," said Rudy.

"What should I do?" asked Chase.

"Well, Robert, you are a congressman for crying out loud and you sit on committees, so do some investigating without raising suspicion. You can do that I hope," Steiner said.

"Stop talking down to me, William. Remember—Rudy and I saved your bacon."

"My bacon, as you put it, was your bacon. I was more like the delivery guy, and Rudy and his dad were the head chefs. You, on the other hand, are more like cooking oil, if you want to stay on the cooking analogy, making sure things will move easily through the red tape. As for Dr. Zimmermann here," Steiner said, turning toward the doctor, "you need to think about taking a trip after that little episode in Oroville. I believe it has made you a person of interest, shall we say."

"I believe you're right, William. I was thinking of a little trip to Canada and then a journey to Latin America, maybe Paraguay. We still have some friends from the old days down there, and a reunion would be nice," Zimmermann agreed.

"Now if we can put the petty squabbles and the vacation planning aside, let's figure out what we should do about the stamp album. It has put Hoffman, Zimmermann, and Steiner in the spotlight. So, Robert and I are the only ones who can remain visible, since we are not in the album. We should be able to deflect any suspicion—as long as the investigation does not go back too far or deep. Even if that is the case, there will be plenty of scrambling by everyone in and outside of the government to cover their asses," said Rudy.

"Does anyone one else have some input?" asked Ernst Hoffmann. But there was no response, so he got up and walked out of the room.

Chapter 56

Passing Arch of Triumph—issued September 28, 1945

September 7, 2001—Seal Beach, California

They were sitting on the bluff looking across the sand and into the water through the gray light of dawn. There were some die-hard surfers out in the water on the north side of the pier.

Most were standing and watching from the parking lot or bluff, either wishing for better conditions or deciding whether to move on down the coast.

A third man sat down with them. "How did you get along?" asked Ernst.

"He is home, and the car was parked in the drive. I placed the device in the right rear wheel well so we should be able to follow him without being spotted. I'll tell you one thing—this guy is dull. All he does is work. And when he's not working, he's reading. The guy buys four newspapers a day. How long are we going to follow him?"

"Until I say we're done. We have to find out what this guy knows and whom he has shared it with. Putting it into U.S. Army slang of World War II, this thing is about to hit the FUBAR level. We need to make sure. I want a report every day from the two of you," Ernst said firmly.

"So we are only to listen to the wire taps and follow his moves?"

"Yes, if an opportunity presents itself for a move into the circle of friends, you are to notify me before any action is taken. Do you both understand?"

The men nodded in agreement.

Werner got up off the bench and walked across the small grass area park. He waited at the light and crossed the street on the green light. On the other side, he stopped at a blue BMW and got in. Looking back across the street, he shook his head and said to himself, "With these two, we'll be lucky if this succeeds." Then he drove off.

On the other side of the street, Carl and Gene watched as the car headed down Pacific Coast Highway.

"What an asshole," said Carl.

"Yeah! Want to go get something to eat?"

"Why not? We've got everything in place, and we can find him anytime we want. Do you want me to drive?"

"Sure. I would have to put the seat back to make room for my legs, and I've got hunger pains. And you like driving anyway."

Carl started the car and turned onto Main Street at the light.

"This place looks like a Norman Rockwell painting. How many towns have diagonal parking these days?" said Gene.

"Not many. I was a kid here right after the war. There was an airstrip on the other side of Pacific Coast Highway, across from the Mahe Restaurant that used to be called the Glider Inn. They kept an old scale model of an airplane on the roof. At the weapons depot, they had these big round balls stacked along PCH, and everyone my age thought they were sea mines to blow up ships. But they were buoys for nets. I was sure disappointed to find out the truth. The real fun was down on the old 'tin can' beach. The state, county, and cities had little to do with the place. There were so many tin cans from the roadside to the water's edge that you had to wear shoes to get to the water. But the parties were wild."

"Why are we stopping here? It's too early for a drink?"

"You said you wanted breakfast, and this place has a good menu. Just don't try to get in on St. Patty's Day."

They got out of the car, walked into the bar, and sat at one of the tall tables by the window.

Chapter 57

Philippines—issued September 27, 1944

The Island of Corregidor is set in the center of the stamp to symbolize the tenacity and courage of the defenders of the Philippines. Controversy unfolded when Filipino officials pointed out that the word "Philippines" is not on the stamp. Others said the drawing of the island was geographically incorrect.

September 8, 2001, at 2:23 a.m.—
Seal Beach, California: things fall apart

The phone rang, and Ernst picked it up.

"It's Carl. The bug we placed in the house is no longer working."

"Why?" asked Ernst.

"Could be a lot of reasons. He might have found it, but I don't think so. He hasn't searched for other bugs. So I think the damn thing just failed," Carl said.

"One of you had better go in and reestablish contact then. We need to keep a close watch on this guy and his friends," said Ernst.

"I'll go. I put the damn thing in there in the first place," Gene said.

"Call back when the job is done," said Ernst. Then he hung up the phone.

Gene turned to Carl, who was sitting next to him in the car. "Stay here," Gene told his partner. "I'll take care of this. He is out of town. And at this time of night, nobody is around. This should only take a few minutes."

Gene opened the car door and stepped into the night air. A cool breeze was coming off the ocean. Walking to the end of the block, he turned at the pier onto the ocean and headed confidently for the house. It was better to have Carl wait in the car. He was too likely to respond impulsively if things got sticky. *That's what happened with that stamp dealer in Oroville, and that's what started this whole mess,* Gene thought.

Bypassing the alarm system took little effort once you knew what you were doing, and Gene had lots of practice installing and bypassing alarm systems. He opened the door, walked into the kitchen, and stopped in his tracks. There was CE, not five feet away, eating a sandwich in the dark.

"Who the hell are you?" asked C.E.

It took a few seconds for this to register with Gene. He reached into his jacket at the same time CE moved toward him. CE kicked out with his right foot, hitting Gene just below his left kneecap. CE had intended to hit the leg and break it. However, he had misjudged the distance, catching the kneecap on the lower side and pushing it up just as Gene pulled out his gun. The gun had a silencer attached, and because of the extra length of the gun barrel, Gene had to slip the gun out carefully so that the barrel did not hang up on his jacket.

As Gene fell to the floor from the dislocated kneecap, he accidentally pulled the trigger, shooting himself just below the left shoulder. Gene hit the floor, his eyes wide in disbelief.

CE reached down and picked up the gun. Then he walked over to the phone on the counter and dialed 911.

Carl, sitting in the car, heard the sirens. He watched as first the fire engine and then a police car, followed by two more police cars and then a paramedic unit, sped in the direction of the house. Carl got out of the car and walked to the corner.

"What the hell happened?" Carl mumbled as he returned to the car to call Ernst. "Ernest, something has gone wrong! There are police, firemen, and paramedic units at the house, and Gene is not back!"

"What do you mean something has gone wrong?"

"Just what I said, something's gone wrong! Gene went to the house to replace the bug. The next thing I know, there are police and medical units all over the place."

"Then go find out what has happened!"

"Are you kidding? The cops are all over the place!"

"There must be neighbors all over the place gawking, so go blend in and see what you can find out."

Carl got out of the car again and walked to the house. Uniformed police were keeping spectators back from the house. Carl moved into the crowd and stood to watch for a minute before he spoke.

"What is happening?" Carl asked of an older man in blue pajamas standing in the group.

"CE shot a burglar in his house, and the police are searching for others," said the man.

"Did anyone die?" asked Carl.

"I don't know. But it looks like CE is okay," the man said, pointing to CE, who was standing next to a police car talking to an officer.

"Wow! Wish I could stay and see what happened, but I've got to go to work in Riverside today. Maybe I'll catch you later to hear the whole story," Carl said, moving slowly away from the crowd. He had seen the police start questioning people and decided it was best if he was not present for questioning.

Chapter 58

**FDR and the Little White House, Warm
Springs, Georgia—issued August 24, 1945**

This was one in a series of stamps commissioned as a tribute to
Franklin Delano Roosevelt.

September 9, 2001, at 4:45 p.m.—New York City

"Here he comes now," Professor Cummings said as he pointed toward Agent Morgan. Wearing a dark-blue suit and white dress shirt with a light blue tie, Morgan was dressed like almost every other male in the building.

"Good to see you, gentlemen," Morgan said, shaking their hands. "Things are coming together rather quickly now since the break-in at your home, CE. Let's talk in my office."

The three men walked over to the elevators and pushed the button. "How is your golf game, Professor? Since I arrived in New York, I have not been able to get many games in. I do get to the driving range at least once a week, but that's not the same."

"My game is just about as good as it was when you used to beat me two out of three times, Albert. You took my money almost every time. Now it's CE who is taking my money, and he does not have the decency that you had to keep the game close. When I play with him and his buddy from the fire department, they steal my ball and make me take a drop."

"I have beaten you once and only by one stroke," CE protested. "And as for stealing your ball, you hit it into the tall grass and then blamed your inability to find it on the two of us, you big cry baby."

The elevator stopped, and the doors opened. A tall redheaded woman dressed in a dark-blue suit was waiting. CE stepped aside and held the door for her.

"Are these the two gentlemen we have been waiting for, Albert?"

"Yes, this is CE Hall and Professor Cummings. This, gentlemen, is my boss, Ms. Madison, and she will be joining us today."

"It is nice to meet you, Ms. Madison," both men said in unison, reaching out to shake her hand.

"The pleasure is mine, gentlemen. And please call me Irene, if you will."

The group stepped inside and entered a small conference room. Irene sat at the head of the rectangular table and invited the men to take a seat.

"Where shall we begin?" she asked, looking at Agent Morgan.

Chapter 59

Deutsches Reich   **Futsches Reich**

(German Empire)   **(Ruined Empire)**

Propaganda Stamps

The single stamp shows Hitler's profile, and he was paid a royalty on each stamp. Block of four portrays the end of the Reich with Hitler's face being eaten away. Operation Cornflake was by OSS & MI before the end of the war January 5, 1954. The Fifteenth US Air Corp targeted a mail train to Linz, and mixed in with the bombs were mailbags filled with forgeries to be part of the debris. A total of 320 mailbags were delivered this way before the war ended.

September 9, 2001—Werner/Moody Group Offices

"We are going to have to close down the Werner/Moody Group as of now. The botched break-in by Carl and Gene has links directly to this organization. So all connections with any of the Werner/Moody group members are terminated as of right now. Those of you who have family connections will need to distance yourselves from the Old Guard," Rudy Werner said.

"That is great for you, Rudy," Congressman Chase complained. "You are sitting behind walls of secrecy while I've been out in front pushing our plans. What am I supposed to do now?"

"Robert, stop playing the victim all the time. You've been out in front with the agenda, but what laws have you broken? We have been protecting you. Your record in the Congress is exceptional. The worst that can be said is that you belonged to an organization that had connections with old Nazis. You can simply say that you had no idea and that you left the organization as soon as you found out," Rudy said. "And some mighty important people will be implicated. They'll be so busy covering their own backsides that they won't have any time to deal with you."

"What can you tell us about the investigation, Robert?" asked Ernst.

"As far as I can tell, Gene died before anyone could question him. He did, however, have his identification and some other items on him that led the detectives to Carl's home. The next day, Carl came home and saw the police at his house. He took off and never returned home."

"What about the album?" asked Rudy.

"That's the rub. Too many eyes have seen it by now," Congressman Chase said. "The Feds are involved, and they have started asking questions to some of the members in the book. It will not be long before they go public with a few individuals to showcase their skills as Nazi hunters. Some of the names in the album will be a major embarrassment to some very important people."

"Damage control is now the order of the day. We need to shut down the organization and distance ourselves from this whole mess,"

Rudy said. He stood up, walked to the door, and opened it for everyone to leave. After the men had exited, he closed the door, locked it, and walked into a nearby office.

"Sorry to keep you waiting, Mohammad," he said to the man waiting in a leather chair. "I was just finishing up some old business."

"Not to worry, Mr. Moody. I am sure we will have a long relationship together."

Chapter 60

SA Mann and SS Mann—issued April 20, 1945

These two stamps were the last stamps issued by the Third Reich in April of 1945.

They were being delivered to postal offices in Berlin while the Red Army was fighting in the city street by street.

September 11, 2001, at 3:00 p.m.—
things change and never change

The day had started with a shock at 8:55 a.m. CE was taking a shower when the phone rang. He grabbed a towel and dried off quickly before he picked up. "Hello?"

"CE, turn on your television right away. A plane just crashed into the north tower of the World Trade Center!" Chief Franklin almost yelled into the phone.

CE turned on the TV just as the second plane hit the south tower. He stood there in disbelief, holding the phone but not saying anything.

.CE hung up the phone and went into his room to get dressed. He was buttoning his shirt when he heard the news reporter say something about the tower. He stepped back into the living room and saw images of a cloud of smoke and dust on the television screen as the south tower crumbled. He watched the footage being replayed again and again. The tower went down in just ten seconds. CE sat down on the couch and listened to the reporters speculate about what was happening. They announced that all air traffic had been grounded. CE was still sitting in front of his television, staring in horror, when a plane hit the Pentagon at 9:37 a.m. and Flight 93 was announced to be missing, possibly a hijacking. The reporters speculated that the White House was its intended target. Unconfirmed reports of the White House being evacuated at 9:48 a.m. were also reported.

CE could not tear himself away from the media coverage. He was still watching at 10:03 a.m., when there were reports that Flight 93 had crashed in Pennsylvania. And at 10:25 a.m., when the north tower collapsed, he put his head in his hands in shock. *In less than two hours, one of America's symbols of world dominance had crumbled,* he thought. *It is just like Pearl Harbor.*

CE turned off the television and headed out to his car. As he drove to his meeting at the federal building, he began to think about the newest attack on the United States. It was different than last time but somewhat the same. This was a radical religious group trying to impose its way of life on the world. They had twisted the beliefs of the Koran to support their vendetta against Western ways and Western beliefs. But they did not live out in the open, like the Nazis did. This group would hide in their caves and spider holes until they were caught or killed.

It was now 3:00 p.m., and CE was waiting in a conference room at the federal building. He was told that Agent Morgan would be there as soon as he could. The day's news had everyone in federal intelligence and law enforcement scurrying to find out what was happening and working to determine what to do next.

A few minutes later, a young woman in a blue business suit with an abundance of blond curly hair poked her head into the room and asked, "Can I get you some coffee or something? Agent Morgan will be with you any minute."

"No, thanks. I'm okay," CE responded.

"Agent Morgan should be with you soon," repeated the woman as she closed the door.

About ten minutes later, the door opened again, and Agent Morgan and another man and woman entered the room.

"I am sorry for making you wait, CE, but today, as you can imagine, has been one of those days."

Agent Morgan shook CE's hand. "I should make some introductions. Ms. Helen Wheeler is my new boss, and this gentleman is Oliver Henry from our financial crimes division. He is a wizard at tracking money."

"It is my pleasure to meet you both," CE said. Then he looked at the man. "I'll bet you get a lot of O' Henry jokes!"

"Not as many as I used to when I was in school," he answered. "I guess most people don't know their American literature anymore. It's a sad shame, though. He was one of America's best authors."

Ms. Wheeler and sat at one end of the table. "Why don't you start, Oliver?"

"I have tracked the money and records as far as I can. The names in the album and quite a few others are in this summary," he said, placing a large file folder on the table. "Some are pretty bad actors, and some are scientists, bureaucrats, and politicians. I have followed the connections as best I could, but most are circumstantial. We don't have a concrete link that will hold up in any court. However, most of the individuals in the album are now dead, and those who are alive will be hard to prosecute, since most of the witnesses are dead."

"Thank you, Oliver. Do you have anything to add, Agent Morgan?" asked Ms. Wheeler.

"No, I have already given you my report, and I think we are ready to proceed."

"Good, then I will send the report over to the Justice Department for further action," Ms. Wheeler said.

"What do you mean further action?" asked CE.

"As I said," Ms. Wheeler repeated, "the report will be handed over to the Justice Department for further action. If you have not noticed, Mr. Hall, the whole nation is in a major crisis that we are trying to get a handle on. We need to spend our time pursuing the people who are currently attacking the United States, not war criminals from many years ago."

"But some of these people are mass murders—or worse! What message does that send to criminals—and to their victims?"

"Mr. Hall, do you know how hard it is to get old cases like this to trial, let alone to get a conviction? You are talking about crimes that were committed over fifty years ago. The time and resources the government has spent to convict Nazis of war crimes is enormous. So we have to set priorities. Right now, our priority is terrorism. The United States has been attacked. That is where we will devote our time and resources." Ms. Wheeler stood up and walked to the door. Then she turned and said, "Thank you, Mr. Hall. Agent Morgan will escort you out." She turned and walked out of the room, followed by Oliver.

"It's a terrible shame," CE said. "I understand the priorities. But what about learning from the past? The Nazis were the terrorists of their day, and they used many of the same tactics. And though we have been teaching the horrors of the Holocaust for fifty years, we still butcher people under a new name—ethnic cleansing. Ordinary people kill their friends, neighbors, and even their family members because of their religion, tribe, or political views. It seems like we haven't learned anything at all from World War II.

"You knew what she was going to say before the meeting started, didn't you?" CE said to Agent Morgan.

"Yes, we had a meeting with her boss just before we came in. Wheeler did not make the decision. It came from higher up the chain of command. She did not like the decision, but that's her job. And for what it's worth, I agree with her decision. We need to protect the people who live in this country right now—and do whatever we can to prevent something like Nazi Germany or what happened today from ever happening again."

Agent Morgan walked CE to the front of the building and shook his hand.

"Look at it this way, CE. We have uncovered the Nazis, and in time, we may have a case against some of the traitors or collaborators. We will prosecute the Nazis in the album who are still alive, if we can locate them, and we'll send them back to their country for prosecution for war crimes. That the best we can do for now."

Agent Morgan waved. Then he turned and walked back into the building.

Later that evening, CE had dinner with Chief Franklin. He shared what had happened at the meeting.

"CE, you are always such a hard head. Remember the time you wrote up the mayor's church for faulty wiring and padlocked exit doors? You gave a letter citing all the violations to the battalion chief, who then gave it to the chief, who tore it up and threw it in the trash can and said you weren't allowed to do inspections on your own anymore. Then the word came back that you were flippant with the minister of that movie star's church, which got you a dressing down by the chief and two days off without pay."

"What is your point?"

"My point is that you need to accept what you can do and not take on what you cannot do, that's all."

"I should give up? Is that what you're saying I should do?" CE said angrily.

"Come on now! Don't get your back up with me. I'm just saying that you need to fight the fights you can win you so will be able to fight another day."

"I don't like it. If it were up to me, these Nazi murderers would be put on trial—even if they were on their deathbeds. Those crimes, and any crimes that involve killing people because of the way they look or what they believe, are heinous. And they will continue until the world holds those responsible accountable for their actions. But the decision is made, and I will have to live with it. The only thing I can be happy about is that some of the bastards will face trial. It may not do much good for the victims, but it will be an acknowledgment of their crimes."

"Yes, I know, CE, and I agree with you. But life goes on. Now can we order our dinner?"

About the Author

D. H. Coop resides in California with his wife, Kay. They have two children and six grandchildren. He was a fire paramedic in Los Angeles County area for eleven years. As the result of a fall at a fire, he worked in the fire prevention bureau for a year and then took a medical retirement. Fortunately, he had a social sciences teaching credential with a major in history, or as he would tell his students, he "fell into teaching." For twenty years he has written as a guest columnist on the subject of history. He drew upon his experiences as a Marine, toolmaker, fire paramedic, fire prevention plan checker, history teacher, avid reader, and a philatelist to write his first historical fiction book, *The Philatelist*.

CPSIA information can be obtained
at www.ICGtesting.com
Printed in the USA
LVHW012103040920
665012LV00004B/88

9 781646 546671